W9-CUH-481

Desert Ghost

Also by Thomas Monroe Helm

TOPANGA'S WOMAN
IRON SKILLET BILL

Desert Ghost

THOMAS MONROE HELM

DOUBLEDAY & COMPANY, INC.
GARDEN CITY, NEW YORK
1977

All of the characters in this book are fictitious, and any resemblance to actual persons, living or dead, is purely coincidental.

Library of Congress Cataloging in Publication Data

Helm, Thomas Monroe, 1917–
Desert ghost.

(A Double D western)
I. Title.
PZ4.H47766De [PS3558.E4767] 813'.5'4
ISBN 0-385-12889-4
Library of Congress Catalog Card Number 76–47819

First Edition

Printed in the United States of America

Desert Ghost

CHAPTER ONE

The two desert men were down in their arrastra sweeping up pulverized quartz with paloverde brooms when the two burros started braying. The burros were good watchdogs. The two men raised up and at once spotted a string of riders and loaded mules a quarter mile out on the playa. Both men were surprised and a little astonished to see men who were obviously not Indians this far out in the desert.

Their vision was partially obstructed in the foreground by ocotillo plants aflame with red blossoms, so they lifted themselves out of the arrastra to get a better look. Baking in the sun-tortured landscape were creosote bush, yucca, agave, saguaro and organpipe cactus, while blue in the distant shimmering haze the peak of Black Hill Four brooded in its corner of the desolate land called the Great American Desert.

From the shade of the saguaro-rib sun shelter nearby the two burros brayed again.

The black man spoke first. "They're coming our way." He was a short man, an inch over five feet, and lean, with peppercorn hair, a second-generation American of African Bushman ancestry. He was naked to the waist and wore a front-and-back-flap breechclout of antelope leather and moccasins with tops reaching up to his knees. His vision was superior to that of his partner, and he was able to make out the features of the horsemen. "Nine white men on mustang horses with seven pack mules." He moved over a few steps to join the burros under the sun shelter.

The white man followed. He too was short, an inch or so taller than his partner, and in addition to similar breechclout and moccasins he wore a vest of antelope hide and a floppy-brimmed buckskin hat. With one arm wrapped around one of the mesquite posts that held up the shelter, he directed his pale blue eyes at the approaching horsemen.

"They look like bandits to me," the white man said. "Nobody else in their right mind would be this far out in the desert in July."

He knew it was July because up till a few days ago they had been harvesting ripe saguaro cactus fruit for boiling in their two-gallon copper kettle for syrup. They had nearly twenty gallons of the tasty syrup stored in saguaro shoes sealed with clay lids and buried three feet underground, where the temperature stayed the same the year round, deep enough so none of the desert creatures could smell it and dig down to get at it.

He continued to stare with some apprehension down the wide arroya, which was flanked by mesquite and paloverde and joshua trees as it meandered southeast toward the playa where they grew their crops of tepary beans and corn and squashes after the winter rains of December and January.

"What do you reckon we ought to do?" he asked.

He asked the question because he was the submissive one of the partnership. He knew and accepted the fact that all workable partnerships are made up of one man who does the camp chores and one man who does the man chores. But it was more than that. He was fully aware from long experience that his partner was by far his superior as a desert man. The little onetime slave with the skinny legs could travel fifty miles a day across the desert on foot and keep it up day after day with a minimum of water. With his bow and his ironwood spears he could run down and kill an antelope. His vision was sharp as that of a hawk and his nose keen enough to smell water under the ground, the same as a coyote. Most important of all, the black man could think. Kestrel Morgan, the white man, at age thirty-one was wise enough to give credit to his brother Snipe Morgan, the black man, where that credit was due.

Snipe took his eyes off the approaching horsemen and glanced up at the saguaro-dotted slope of Black Hill Three. "I'll take the bow and the spears up the hill and you stay to talk with them. Pretend I'm armed with a rifle. We don't have anything to tempt nine bandits, but there's no sense taking chances. If they are bandits, they're out for bigger game than a pair of poor desert prospectors."

He shifted his purple-grape-colored eyes back to the horsemen. "I see water kegs on the mules. Don't wait for them to ask for water. Give them the freedom of the spring." He grinned encouragement at his partner, knowing that he was not a courageous man, and went to the dome-shaped grass-covered hut for his bow and spears and spear-throwing stick before heading up the slope.

Because they were both small of stature and appeared easy to lick, the two men often resorted to guile and trickery. They were both the same age and had been friends and partners all of their lives. They had come west from Alabama seven years before to earn their fortunes. For a year they had been employed as scouts by the Army and had learned some of the ways of the Apaches. Not being able to save a fortune as scouts, they had become prospectors, and had chosen the desert because most other prospectors did not.

This area where they were now, on the south slope of Black Hill Three, they had visited many times over the years because of the spring and because they used the playa as their garden. But it wasn't until some six months ago that they had discovered the vein of gold-bearing quartz. Since then they had built their sleeping shelter, patterned after the huts of the Papago Indians, the sun shelter that shaded their kitchen midden, and the arrastra.

They had worked four batches of ore in the arrastra and had discovered that the quartz was rich, running at a guess nearly two ounces of gold to the ton. They had struck a bonanza, but of late they had agreed that getting the ore out with only a sledge and a cold chisel and working it in the arrastra would take five years or more to earn the ten thousand dollars apiece that they had set as their goal. What they needed was a small crusher run by a steam engine and a dry washer, along with a goodly supply of blasting powder and a pound of quicksilver, and those items they knew would be costly.

For a month they had talked about traveling north to the mining town of Prospect, a distance of about a hundred miles, and there asking the town banker for a loan. With the proper equipment, they estimated that they could take out twenty thousand dollars worth of gold in six months. They were no longer young men; they did not have five years to spare, so they had planned to leave as soon as they finished sweeping up the pulverized quartz ore that they now had in the arrastra. They held no doubts that the banker would grant them a loan when he saw the richness of the ore they would show him.

The horsemen were closer now, climbing up the lower slope not a hundred yards away. The men looked to Kestrel almost as big as the tough little mustangs they were riding. It was obvious that they had spotted him as well as the sun shelter and the hut. The two burros beside him had their ears cocked. To his right the sun was three fingers high, a ball of fire in a sky unmarked by even the faintest speck of cloud.

He thought about the small leather poke of gold dust buried near the door of the hut. About five ounces. Not much, but it was more gold than they'd seen in the past six years. The vein of quartz around on the east side of the hill was narrow, about five inches wide between some hard country rock. He made a decision to volunteer the location of the mine rather than be closemouthed about it. More guile.

He could see faces now, and they looked mean as bobcats. He stepped slowly out from under the shelter and stood in the sun, forcing a smile to his face. "Howdy!" he called out cheerfully.

The lead horseman came on to within twenty yards and drew his horse to a halt. With one sweeping glance he took in the hut, the shelter, the burros and the arrastra. A bob of his head and he said, "Where's your partner, mister?"

"He's up on the hill. Hop down and rest a spell out of the sun. Can't offer you coffee because we ain't got none. Plenty of water though. Help yourself. Spring's over yonder a piece by that fan palm. Don't bother the pair of chulas up the tree. They're pets. Least they are till we get hungry enough." He was referring to a pair of coatimundis that lived in the fan palm. Because of all the desert creatures they had left the spring clear, building over here a distance away. The spring was not a heavy producer; it gave only about three gallons an hour this time of year, but by building a dam around the pool they were able to hold all they and the desert creatures needed.

Looking up at the man, Kestrel was reminded that he had a year's growth of whiskers himself. He hoped he didn't look as mean as this one though. The man had a brush of black whiskers bushy enough to sweep the arrastra with. The other riders had stopped and were waiting, their eyes looking around with disdain at the poorness of the camp. As the big man stepped down from his saddle, he made a gesture at the other men and they rode on toward the fan palm and the spring.

Kestrel kept grinning like an idiot as he watched the

string of mules go by; each of them carried four ten-gallon kegs, a heavy load for any mule. The kegs looked as if they might have held whiskey at one time. He dismissed the notion that they might still hold whiskey—there were no Indians anywhere nearby worth trading with. The only Indians he knew about were a tribe of Papagos over near Ironwood Hill, and the Papagos didn't have anything even worth stealing but a few tepary beans and some saguaro syrup. He remembered that the Papagos would be celebrating the saguaro-harvest moon along about now. In about another ten days anyway.

The big whiskery man took a position in front of Kestrel and said, "What's your partner doing up the hill, mister?"

"Oh, he's just up there doing nothing."

"He got a gun?"

"Yes, indeed he has, mister. A great big old Sharps buffalo gun. Blow a hole through a steam locomotive with it." Kestrel kept right on grinning.

The mean old hombre lifted one eyebrow and pushed down one corner of his lips. He pointed a hairy finger at the arrastra. "How you making out?"

"Bacon and beans is about all. Just got started. The mine's around the side of the hill. My name's Morgan by the way. Kestrel Morgan from Alabama." He was still apprehensive but he couldn't sense any reason to be afraid, not yet anyhow.

The man produced a skinny cigar that looked like a crooked stick and a block of lucifers. With the cigar in his jaw he struck a lucifer and lit up. "How far is it up to Thimble from here?"

"Thimble? I'd say a right far piece, mister. A hundred miles, give or take."

"Any water along the way?"

"Some. Not a hell of a lot this time of year. Some though, if you know where to look for it."

The man fixed him with a look that would bore a hole in an ironwood tree. "How about you telling me where to look then."

"Be glad to, mister," Kestrel said cheerfully. "A man could dry up to a sliver without water out here." He looked around near his feet and picked up a creosote stick. Hunkering down, he used the stick to draw a map. "Say you're right here now. One Palm Spring. This hill we call Black Hill Three because there's four hills just about all alike running south to north. You passed Black Hill Four back a piece. That's her down yonder. Well, Black Hill Two is up here about ten miles. Then it's another ten miles or so to Black Hill One." He drew four oblong circles in a row.

"You won't find any water on Two and One. But over here about ten miles to the west of Two you'll find a great big hill of bull quartz. On the other side, that's the west side, you'll find some fan palms and a good spring. You'll be going northwest, so Bull Quartz Spring is right on your way. Now, a little farther on, say about thirty miles, you'll come to a deep gorge. Oh, I'd say it's all of thirty feet deep most spots. Runs northeast to southwest. Can't miss it. Fall in and break your neck if you ain't careful. Anyway, along the gorge there's some tanks the Papagos dug in solid rock.

"Now, if you're headed straight for Thimble, there ain't

no more water between the gorge and there. Not this time of year anyhow. You got all that?" Kestrel knew he wouldn't give wrong directions or wrong information to anybody in the desert, not even his worst enemy, but he didn't say as much.

The man studied the map while Kestrel studied the man. He was a hefty, tough-looking hombre, wearing a big Mexican-style hat and a Navy Colt revolver in addition to a new-looking model '73 Winchester rifle crooked in his left elbow. Kestrel envied him the rifle; he and Snipe had never found enough gold to buy one. The man had bandit written all over him. A successful bandit too. His boots were new and looked like they might have cost fifty dollars. Kestrel didn't envy him the boots. If he had to walk in boots like that, he'd be a cripple in a mile on the desert pavement.

"Is there any town closer than Thimble? What's in this direction? East of Thimble."

"Nothing but desert, mister. For sixty miles anyway."

"That would be closer to here. What's the name of the place? Any water between here and there?"

"Prospect. Mining town. Some ranches. Some farms. Good-size town, too. Bet they got three, maybe four hundred people. Me and my partner ain't been up there for a couple of years."

As the man raised up, Kestrel wondered why the man had got down off his horse toting the rifle when he had a pistol on his hip. Habit, most likely. He saw the man look up the slope and shift the cigar in his jaw. "Well, much oblige, mister. We'll be riding on."

"Drop by any time, mister," Kestrel said. "Always glad

to see folks. We might have us some coffee next time you come by."

The piercing look again. "What makes you think we'll be coming by again?"

"Not a thing, mister. Not a thing. Just being mannerly is all." Kestrel had been about to suggest in a friendly way that it would be best for the man to travel at night this time of year, that the heat of the desert pavement under the hoofs of the horses would cripple them, the heat working up the leg and cooking the marrow in the bone, but he held his tongue because of the man's tone of voice.

A minute later the bandits were gone, out of sight around the east side of the hill. Kestrel knew that Snipe wouldn't come down from the hill until he got a signal, so he strolled over to the spring. The catch basin was almost dry, with only about a sip of water left in the bottom. The men and horses and mules had drunk it dry. He looked up at the two chulas and said howdy. The strange-looking animals, a cross between a monkey and a raccoon, so it seemed, stayed up in the tree during the daylight to escape the heat. It was a lot cooler up there ten feet off the ground.

Then he strolled on east of the spring until he could see the tail end of the last mule. As the string made a zig to the right on the trail, he counted nine horsemen and seven mules—none left behind to do mischief. Good riddance, he thought, and went back to the shelter and signaled to Snipe.

While Snipe was coming down from the hill, Kestrel took a Papago basket to a mesquite tree and picked about two pounds of the long bean pods. He returned to the kitchen midden, built a fire by using his flint and steel, and put the beans on to cook, pods and all. They'd been out of lucifers for many months, so long that he now thought nothing about using the old-fashioned way of making fire. Later he would add some antelope jerky to the beans for flavoring and that with some corn tortillas and some saguaro-fruit syrup would be their supper. Having mentioned coffee to the bandit made him hanker for some coffee. He couldn't remember the last time he'd had some coffee. The reason he'd mentioned it to the bandit was a hope the man would give him a handful. Stingy old goat.

When Snipe came down from the hill, they speculated a bit about the bandits. "If I was living in Thimble, along about five, six days from now I'd sure lock up the money jar if I had a money jar," Kestrel said.

"That's where they're headed, eh?"

"That's what he said. No, take that back. All he did was ask how far it is, to Thimble that is. Asked about Prospect too. No he didn't. He asked if there was a town to the east of Thimble and I told him about Prospect. Told him about Bull Quartz Spring and the tanks along the gorge. Big Gorge, over west of Bull Quartz. Anyway, he's gone. And thank the Lord for that. I come dang near asking him straight out for some coffee and he never said a word. Stingy old goat. Was about to tell him about traveling at night 'stead of in the hot sun but he bore a hole in me with his eyes so I snapped my jaw shut. He sure did believe you had you a rifle up there. Big old buffalo gun, I told him. Sharps. Blow a hole in a steam locomotive. Not that he was about to do anything. He's after big game all right enough. Beans on cooking. Mesquite. Best to save the teparies cause the mesquites won't be on the trees much longer green in the pod the way we like 'em. Could do with some fresh meat. You up to getting us a rabbit or two?"

"Sure." Snipe took his bow and one arrow to go off after a rabbit down the wash.

While Snipe was gone, Kestrel swept up the rest of the pulverized quartz in the arrastra and shoveled it up with a small shovel he'd whittled out of a chunk of ironwood. It had taken him a month of whittling to make the shovel. It wasn't much bigger than his hand. Not that he minded the time spent. Wasn't nothing else to do. They could use a real iron shovel though. Could use a lot of things, he was thinking.

The shoveling done, he went back to the sun shelter and stirred the beans, putting more wood under the pot. In the sun it was so hot he could drop a drop of water from waist high and it would be evaporated before it could hit the ground. He sat down under the shelter to wait for Snipe.

"How much you reckon a small crusher with a small steam engine would cost us?" Kestrel asked for the hundredth time when Snipe came in with a jackrabbit that looked as tough as the boss bandit.

"We agreed on a thousand dollars at least, didn't we?"

"Yeah. I figure all of that much. Lot of money to us, but it ain't much for a bank. We'd be a whole year earning a thousand dollars the way we're going. What say we head up to Prospect and tackle that banker?"

"That suits me," Snipe said. "When do you want to leave? Tonight?"

"Well. We ain't in that big a hurry."

Snipe smiled. They'd been on the verge of leaving almost every evening for the past ten days, ever since they made the last cleanup of the arrastra. He decided he'd nail Kestrel down. "All right. Tonight it is."

Kestrel stroked his whiskers. "It'll take a bit of getting ready, Snipe. I've got to grind some corn to take along and fill the water gourds."

"The water gourds are already filled, partner."

"They are? All hundred of them?"

"All one hundred and six."

"Oh? Well, in that case I reckon we can—" Kestrel worried his whiskers and looked up at the sky. He couldn't think of anything else they had to do.

"You finish supper and grind the corn and I'll get the burros loaded." Snipe was grinning. "We'll leave soon as the sun goes down."

"Sure. Sure." Kestrel muttered to himself and sauntered over to look down in the arrastra and came back to the shelter. He was a stay-put sort of man, and as Snipe knew, it took some doing to get him started. Kestrel stopped and looked back over one shoulder hopefully. "We ought to take along some ore samples, you know."

"I'll go around and get some, partner." Snipe laughed. They could laugh at each other without hurt feelings because they had been partners for a lot of years and forgave each other their faults.

CHAPTER TWO

After he left the grinning jackass who lived like a root digger, Gower Blount led his band around the hill and set a course north toward Black Hill Two, which he could see in the distance. He was in no great rush. What he was after wouldn't go away. It was good to savor what he was about to do to his longtime enemy. He had planned this venture for years and it had taken a lot of doing to get the money together and a lot of talking to get the eight men to join him. They were not the men he would have liked—a bunch of losers taken from the dregs of Santa Fe, the sort of men too lazy or too dumb to do for themselves. But they'd have to do.

George Wakefield. He felt his teeth grind at the mere thought of the man. Wakefield, who had stolen his wife and his land. Well, his wife's land, which was the same thing. That had been a long time ago, right after the war. Then Wakefield sold out and left Valdosta to move West, and it had taken him until a year ago to track the man down. Big-shot banker he was now, fat and sassy, the king of Prospect. He had it all figured out; the man he'd sent to Prospect had found out all he needed to know.

The house, the bank, the town marshal, how the little girl went to the bank every day to take her old man's dinner. First he'd kill the woman, then he'd take Wakefield's money, every penny of it, then he'd take the little girl. He could kill Wakefield, but then the man's agony and suffering would be over. No profit there. He wanted revenge and he meant to get it. Then Wakefield would know what it's like to start anew without a penny. The bank's depositors would demand their money, and Wakefield would be forced to sell his land and his house and his half interest in the Lucky Emily Mine, maybe even his pants.

He thought it a pity that he wouldn't be around to witness his enemy's downfall. Still, he could send his man back to Prospect to observe and let him know. By then he'd have plenty of money. Wakefield's money.

His horse clipped a forehoof and stumbled. He yanked the animal up and lifted his hat to dry-wash his face. He'd downed a gallon of water minutes ago and already he was parched. Miserable country. But it was this desert that would save his neck in a few days. A posse wouldn't be able to tote enough water to give chase and catch him. He began looking ahead for a place to camp. The sun was about down; time to call it a day. They'd come a good twenty miles since daybreak. Hot going. The land ahead was flat, as almost all of this desert was flat except for the scattered black hills that seemed to have grown out of the flatness like big fat beetles. He'd been seeing the same kind of bushes and small trees and cactus plants for the past six days. An endless nothing.

Up ahead and to his right stood a giant saguaro with three arms. A good place to put up a white marker.

They'd never find the spots where the kegs were buried without the markers, not if it happened to rain. That would cook his gander, if it should rain in the next day or two after they held up the bank. But it wouldn't rain; a man in Santa Fe who knew the desert had told him that in this part of the desert it only rained during the winter months. Down south there were summer showers, but not up here.

He saw a redtailed hawk perched atop the saguaro. Around the giant cactus were the usual ocotillo and agave and cholla. He turned in his saddle to look back at the men. Every eye was fixed on him. They knew who the boss was. He raised his hand and called back, "Camp up ahead."

Blount dismounted near the three-armed saguaro and motioned to the man called Hobart, whom he liked to think of as his segundo but he didn't call him that. Hobart was a man of fifty who had been a sergeant in the Confederate Army and liked to be called sergeant, not segundo. He was the bossy type who never let the men use their own judgment; when he gave orders he gave them in detail as if the men couldn't think for themselves.

"Take charge, sergeant. Bury four kegs and open two."

"Boss, we ain't more than ten miles north of that spring back there. We'll need water farther up more than we'll need it down here."

"We won't be stopping at the spring on the way back, sergeant. Bury the kegs and hook one of the flags high up on this cactus."

Hobart tugged at his whiskers and kicked at the ground, a sign that something wasn't to his liking. "Boss, the men want to know where they're going. You said you'd tell them when we got halfway. Well, we ought to be halfway, the way I figure it."

"After we eat, sergeant. That'll be all."

"Right, boss." Hobart turned to the men, who had gathered around. "Moss, you and Kelly dig a hole. Forty, you and Jerome cook up some grub. Stump, you and Magpie and Joe Brown unload the mules and hobble the horses." He took a white rag from his saddlebag and got the long pole from one of the pack mules and used it to lift the rag high and impale it on the spines of the saguaro. Like all of the larger saguaros he'd seen, this one had a dozen woodpecker holes high up. He saw the head of an elf owl in one hole; and atop the plant a flicker perched, fussing down at the intruders.

Blount watched the men to see how they were holding up. They looked like so many sheep blindly following a Judas goat. Fourteen-year-old Joe Brown and the two cowhands, Kelly and Jerome—both also just boys in their teens—were holding up well enough because of their youth. Old Stump Brown looked all petered out and was being grumpy with his son, who was too friendly and trusting to suit Blount's taste. He'd have to keep an eye on Joe. Too tenderhearted. Liable to balk when the time came for action.

He had guaranteed the eight men a hundred dollars in gold coin each to help him with the upcoming caper. He'd told them they were going to rob a bank, but he didn't tell them where. That he'd kept to himself for fear that if he had told them sooner one might back out and take a notion to tell the law. He didn't trust any of them;

but the men seemed to trust Hobart. He supposed it was because the ex-sergeant didn't hesitate to give orders. The men were the kind that had to be told what to do and how to do it. A sorry lot.

After they had eaten, Blount had Hobart call the men together. When they had settled down around the cookfire, he said, "I told you in Santa Fe that we were going to rob a bank, and you all agreed to go along. What I didn't tell you was what bank. Well, it's the bank in a town called Prospect. We'll be there in four days. I've had a man there looking things over for the past six months, so you can see I know what I'm doing. There won't be any trouble. We'll go in and out in less than an hour.

"Now, the banker's name is Wakefield. The teller's name is Percy Potter. Both men are in their forties and they don't tote guns. The town marshal's an old man of sixty or so and he does tote a gun. His name is Bill Butterworth. The marshal goes home to his wife for his dinner every day at noon and he lives out of town about a mile, on the east end of town. At ten minutes past noon is when we hit the bank. The banker eats his dinner inside the bank. His daughter fetches it to him. We go in immediately after the daughter goes in."

He paused. "Anybody wants to pull out, now's the time to do it. Just remember that if you do, you leave your horse here and it's a long way to walk back to Yucca Flat."

He saw Stump Brown look at his son, who shrugged his shoulders as if to say, We're stuck, Pa. The others looked around at each other and said nothing.

Blount went on. "From all the information my man

could gather there'll be somewhere between twenty and forty thousand dollars in the bank, most of it in gold coin. The banker hasn't got around to having his own banknotes printed, which is a good thing because they'd be worthless to us. Twenty thousand in gold is a lot of weight, so I'll need four men with me inside the bank, four men who're not afraid to use their guns if they have to." He looked at Hobart. "Sergeant?"

"Count me in."

"I'll go," said the old man called Magpie.

"Two more. What about you, Moss?" Moss looked mean enough to shoot his mother.

"I've never shot a man, boss," Moss said.

So much for looks, Blount thought. "How about you, Forty Acre Smith?"

"I'll go, but I want more money."

"How does an extra five hundred sound?"

"No matter how much or how little we take?"

"That's right."

"Count me in then."

"One more."

One of the cowhands, the tall, rawboned boy called Jerome, said, "For five hundred extra I'll go in with you, boss. But I figure we ought to get a cut of the take besides a measly hundred. Who gets all that twenty to forty thousand—you?"

Blount had been expecting this to happen. Give a beggar your coat and he wants your wallet. "All I get is half," he said. "The rest you can divide up among you. All right. Me, Hobart, Forty, Magpie, and Jerome go in. Stump, you and Moss and Kelly will take your rifles and stand in front of the Mercantile Store across the street from the bank. You can't miss the bank. It's on the southeast corner of Main Street and Valley Road. There's other stores along Main Street, so don't pick the wrong store. Joe Brown will be holding the horses on Valley Road on the west side of the bank.

"Now, we hit the bank at ten past noon. I've got a watch here." He pulled it out to show it to them. "I'll let Hobart hold my watch because I'm going into town about an hour ahead of you. I'll be at the bank before you get there. Now, my watch might not have the same time they keep in Prospect. It might be twenty minutes to a half hour off either way. So go in and get set at eleven-forty by my watch. You got that, sergeant?"

"Right. I got it, boss. We'll be at the bank at eleven-forty and wait for you. That's twenty minutes before noon."

He was expecting somebody to ask why he was going in an hour ahead, but nobody did.

"That's correct, sergeant. Now, after we come out of the bank, we'll ride south, right back into the desert. We'll ride hard for about ten miles. Then we'll slow down and save the horses."

"The horses are already pretty much tuckered out, boss," Forty Acre Smith, the muleskinner, said. "They can't run no ten miles. Better make that three miles. Four at the most."

"Good thought, Forty. Four miles it will be then. We'll bury the last two water kegs about eight or ten miles out of town. The buried water is what will guarantee our escape. Any posse without a lot of water along will have to turn back after the first day, so for the first thirty miles or so we'll have to move fast." He wanted to tell them that they would not have any posse on their tails because of the little girl, but he was afraid to tell them about her. Sometimes even the most brutal of men will draw back from doing harm to children. "I guess that's about it."

"What about the mules, boss?"

"Good point. We'll stake out one mule ten miles south of town with the grub and gear. The others we'll abandon the way we've been doing it. Any more questions?" When none was forthcoming, he said, "That's it then. You have three days to think about it. We'll stay together back across the desert and then split up at Yucca Flat." He rose to his feet as an elf owl went twit-twit, and motioned to Hobart to join him. Together they drew away from the campfire, out with the hobbled horses and mules.

Blount had known Hobart for about forty days. He first met the stiff-backed ex-sergeant in a saloon in Santa Fe. Together they had recruited the others. To get Hobart to go along with him, he'd had to tell him the full plan, all but where the bank was located and the part about taking the banker's daughter. Now he wanted to find out whether Hobart would go along with taking the girl. He didn't intend to tell anybody about his plan to kill the snippy-nosed Mrs. Emily Wakefield.

With his back to the campsite and standing near a mule hungrily cropping foliage from a mesquite tree, Blount said, "How do you feel about the others, sergeant?"

"They ain't fit, boss." Hobart shook his head. "If I had a few months to whip them into shape maybe they'd do. But even then they'd still be saloon sweepings."

Blount inclined his head. "How would you take to splitting up their shares two ways. Just you and me."

"I'll be earning it anyway. Might as well take it and be done with the fuss. What you got in mind?"

"Well, I want to take the banker's daughter. That way there won't be any posse. If they chase us, we'll threaten to kill the girl. Sort of an ace in the hole, you might say."

"Now I don't take to hurting young'ns, boss. You ain't fixing to hurt her none, are you?"

"Certainly not," Blount lied. "We'll turn her loose when we get to Yucca Flat."

"Well, in that case I reckon it's all right. What do we do with the seven men?"

"What would you suggest, sergeant?"

"You just leave it to me, boss. I'll figure out something."

"Very well, then. We'll talk more about it later on." Blount paused for a moment and gave Hobart one of his cigars. "You're a good man, sergeant. Maybe we can do something else together after this."

"Maybe," and Hobart eased off back to the camp.

CHAPTER THREE

The sun was one finger high in the west when Snipe put the packsaddles on the two jenny burros and hung four large heavyweight canvas bags on them. Into each bag he put twenty-six water gourds. He and Kestrel had grown the gourds themselves out on the playa after the winter rains of two springs ago. These gourds had the right shape, fat bellies and slender necks. The tops of the necks had been cut off and stoppers made out of dry barrel cactus pulp. They had shaped the dry pulp just right for each gourd, inserted them into the necks, and uptilted the gourds, so that the pulp would swell up and become watertight.

Snipe felt that his old dad, the Bushman captured in Africa when he was a young man and brought to the slave market at Mobile in 1847, would approve of him now. He and Kestrel had become almost entirely self-sufficient here in the desert. Almost everything they owned they had made themselves. They had made the two packsaddles out of mesquite wood, shaping each piece with hatchet and knife and tying them together with wet antelope hide. The belly straps were made out of yucca fibers, as were the ropes and the halters. The canvas they had taken from a derelict covered wagon they had come upon far to the west four years ago. Around the wagon they had found four piles of bones—a man, a woman, and two children, dead of thirst most likely—along with the bones of two horses still hitched to the wagon tongue.

They had spent scarcely fifty dollars during the past six years of roaming over the desert. They had not even bought the two jenny burros. Traveling far to the west the same year they found the wagon, as far as the great gorge now being called the Grand Canyon, they had found a herd of the wild burros the desert Indians had told them about. By running after the young burros in relays, very much as wolves chase their prey, they had run down the two little jennies, at the time no older than two months. They had gentled the little beasts until now they were pets that never strayed. They had chosen jenny burros intentionally, for they had been told that jack burros tend to stray. Recently, while building the arrastra and needing heavy chains to drag the abrasive stones, they had gone back to the derelict wagon to take the trace chains.

Over the years they had adopted the ways of those gentle desert people the Papagos. Their night shelter was the dome-shaped hut formed by mesquite posts covered with bundles of coarse grass held in place by hoops of ocotillo stems. They tanned antelope skins for their Apache style moccasins and their simple garments and hats. They subsisted on foods they grew themselves out on the playa after the winter rains—corn, squash, tepary beans. They harvested the fruit of the saguaro and boiled the flesh for syrup. For meat they killed deer, antelope, javalina pigs, rabbits, and snakes. They trapped the desert quail. They lived about as well as any man can live in the desert, but it was a way of life that did not satisfy their souls, for they had no women. The kind of women they someday hoped to have would not embrace the desert life.

More and more now as the days and months and seasons flowed by, they talked about what they wanted to do. It was Kestrel's ambition to return someday to Alabama a rich man, there to buy a farm and build a house and find a woman. Snipe's ambition was similar with the difference that he wanted to own a ranch somewhere below the border, where all men were respected for their worth and not for the color of their skins. After many long evenings of talk when the western sky turned mauve and pink and then purple, they had estimated that to satisfy their dreams they would each need at least ten thousand dollars. Now, with the discovery of the rich vein of gold quartz, they could see ahead the fulfillment of their dreams.

Into one canvas bag, on top of the water gourds, Snipe put a leather pouch full of ore samples. The moccasin-patching pouch. He added the hatchet, the iron skillet when Kestrel was finished with it, and a bag of antelope jerky.

He balanced the bags with four saguaro shoes filled with syrup. Saguaro shoes are so hard and durable they often last for a hundred years after the parent plant died, so the Papagos had told them. They can be found in every large dead saguaro. The shoes are the remains of woodpecker nests. When the bird pecks out a hole in the sanguaro, down into the fleshy pulp often to a depth of ten or more inches, the plant heals its wound with a secretion that hardens to the consistency of rock. Then when the plant dies, the nests continue to endure for many years. The Papagos had shown Snipe the shoes and had told him of their uses. They could be made watertight by cementing a flat piece of clay over the original opening the bird had once used.

Snipe had three ironwood spears, each seven feet long, tipped with volcanic rock points made fast with deerhide strips. He tied them, along with the throwing stick, to one burro's pack and encased the points with leather sheaths to prevent the burro from wounding herself by chance. The throwing stick was four feet long with a leather pocket at one end that fit over the butt end of the spears. It was used to give velocity and distance to the throw. On the other burro's pack he made fast his bow and a quiver with about two dozen arrows. He separated the two weapons so that in the event one burro was stolen by a hostile redskin or whiteskin he would still have a weapon to fight with.

When he had everything packed that he thought they would possibly need, he led the burros to the spring and let them drink all they could hold. He knew that the little beasts could survive in the desert for as long as twenty days without actually drinking water for they could subsist on desert succulents. The trek to the town of Prospect he estimated would take four nights. Nights because he would never travel the hot desert during the daylight hours. Only fools and ignorant white men do that.

"Did I forget anything?" Snipe asked of Kestrel, who had a better mind for remembering the little things—and it was the little things that could kill you in the desert.

"Flint and steel?"

"I would have gone off without them." Snipe scooped up a bite of mesquite beans with a tortilla. "I like the tepary beans a lot better than these mesquites."

"You always say that. Well, next year we'll simply plant more teparies. Try the rabbit. I boiled hell up to it before roasting. The gold poke?"

"Shoot!" and Snipe went over to the hut to dig up the gold poke before he could forget it again.

"When we get to Prospect, we'd better buy us some California pants and shirts before we tackle the banker. He'll think we're a pair of blanket Indians in these duds. Take your hat along."

"I guess I'd better."

"Got your knife?"

"Yep."

"Well, I guess that's it then. I'll load in the drinking mugs and the big and little pots. Water reeds?"

"Those I never forget." Snipe raised his baked clay mug and swallowed some joint-fir tea. The water reeds were hollow willow branches an inch in diameter and each about thirty inches long. They used them to suck up water out of damp sand. Snipe's Bushman dad had taught him the trick of using a reed long years ago and they had used a reed in the desert several times. One time a reed had actually saved their lives. Hence his saying that he would never forget them.

When everything was loaded into the canvas bags,

Snipe tied down the packs with yucca-fiber rope and they left the camp, each of them looking back when they were ten or so feet along as if they wanted to imprint a picture of it on their memories.

It was sunset.

Snipe led the way with the more dominant burro in tow on a lead rope; the second burro followed along without need of a rope. Kestrel brought up the rear. When they were around the hill on the east side, Snipe set a course one fingerwidth to the east of the North Star and set a leisurely pace that would average about three miles every hour.

The July twilight lasted for about an hour, followed by about five hours of starlit darkness, then dawn began. They continued on until just before sunup and stopped to camp beside a dry wash flanked by joshua and mesquite trees. They had come a bit over twenty-five miles, to Snipe's reckoning.

They chose a spot on the west side of a large joshua tree and, while Kestrel unloaded the burros and emptied six of the water gourds into the big copper pot for the burros to drink, Snipe took his bow and went hunting for breakfast meat. He returned in a few minutes with a big rattlesnake that had been night hunting and had captured a pack rat. They were both fond of snake meat, not only rattlesnake but other snakes as well; it was a desert delicacy. Kestrel chopped the snake's head off, skinned it, cleaned out the pack rat and entrails, and cut it in three-inch lengths to roast on sticks. He made tortillas in the iron skillet and boiled tea in the small pot. After eating, they settled down in the shade to sleep.

The burros browsed on nearby mesquite foliage and

beans and topped it off with some prickly-pear cactus pads. Then they moved over to the shade by the sleeping men and dozed on their feet. At midday both men and burros moved around to the east side of the shade tree. They drank water often, for the day was a scorcher, dry and hot enough to cook a man's brains. During the afternoon Kestrel put on a pot of tepary beans to cook, and just before sunset they ate supper and broke camp as the sun was setting.

By sunrise of the fourth night they were in sight of Prospect. The mining town was located at the mouth of a long, wide valley, close to the eastern hills. Up on the side of the hill were mine-shaft openings and mine buildings. They counted seven tailing slides.

"You know something, Snipe," Kestrel said as they continued toward the town. "We might be able to buy the very crusher we need right here instead of sending back to St. Louis or Chicago for it."

"Be handy if we can," Snipe agreed. "Place is a lot bigger than it was when we were here last. Must be a hundred houses besides the stores. And look at that big building; looks like a stamp mill. Sure it is; I can hear the crushers all the way out here. Seven mines up on the hill that we can count. That hill must be solid gold ore. Quite a town, Kes. How'd you like to live here?"

"Not for me, old buddy. I don't like towns and you don't either. You'll be down in Mexico a year from now, riding around your big ranch. Wonder what it'll be like. You know, if our ore holds out, we might take a fortune. Ten thousand apiece easy. Maybe a lot more. It's mighty rich ore."

"First we catch us a crusher, Kes." Snipe grinned back

at his partner. "Like they say about rabbit stew. What say we put the girls in a stable and buy us some new duds and get shaved and our hair cut and tackle that banker today?"

"Sooner the better for me."

They went on into town and stopped at the watering trough in front of the Prospect Mercantile Store. As they were climbing up to the store porch, Kestrel turned to look around and saw a tall man wearing a fancy black suit and a derby hat go into the bank across the street.

CHAPTER FOUR

On Wednesday, the twenty-seventh of July, 1881, when he went down to breakfast, George Wakefield said to his daughter, "Morning, honey. I do believe it's time I got you a pony."

As he kissed his wife and sat down, the little girl, who was wearing red-cotton long pants and a yellow cowboy shirt and who wouldn't be caught asleep in a dress, threw herself at her father and yelped, "When! When, Daddy! When!"

In her boy's outfit complete with cowboy boots, she looked like a boy. Her yellow hair was bobbed short and a splotch of freckles was painted across the bridge of her tiptilted nose.

Her long-suffering mother, plump but still pretty at age forty-one, who had a trunkful of little-girl dresses she'd have to give away soon, threw up her hands and cried, "Lord save us!" Still, she smiled at her husband, whom she adored. Then she called out toward the kitchen, "Hazel. You can fetch in the grub now." The word grub was for her daughter's benefit.

The father was untangling skinny arms from around his

neck as the hired girl brought in a platter of fried ham and fried eggs. "Grits and biscuits coming up." And back to the kitchen she went wearing a pleased grin on her homely face.

"When, Daddy?"

"Wal, old girl," the father said, trying with little success to drawl like a real cowboy, "I do reckon today's the day we give away little girls with every pound of cake." It was part of a nursery rhyme, but he couldn't remember which one.

"Oh, Daddy!" and again he was showered with wet kisses. "When today?"

George Wakefield shook out his napkin, tucked one corner in his collar, and reached for the coffee pot. "This afternoon, honey. Hank Hannibal will fetch him in to the bank sometime after noon. Now you sit and eat your grub."

Libby knew when to be good. She obediently sat down even though her excitement was almost more than she could bear. "What color is he, Daddy? Have you seen him? Have you, Daddy?"

Her father spooned a dollop of grits onto her plate, added an egg on top, and speared a slab of ham, which he began cutting into mouth-size bites for her. He knew very well that she was too old to have her meat cut for her but he couldn't break the habit. "He's brown with white spots and he's got three white stockings. Now eat."

Libby couldn't help saying, "Daddy, I do wish you'd stop cutting up my meat for me." Then she added a soft "Please."

"I will if you'll promise not to pick it up with your

fingers and bite off chunks like a little savage." He winked at his wife, who was beaming at them both. "By the way," he said to her, "I've decided to lend Hank the money to buy those fancy cows and the bull he wants."

"That's nice, dear. Maybe in a few years we'll be able to buy beef we won't have to cut with a hatchet."

"They're called cattle, Daddy, not cows."

"Oh?" He lifted an eyebrow at her. He was a handsome man, a little portly, but a little extra suet, as his wife called it, he considered becoming to a banker. "Well, honey, if you had two cattle and took away one, how many cattle would you have left? One cattle?" He laughed. "But you're right, honey. I'm still the Georgia man. Back there we call cows cows." He looked at his wife. "Shall we count our blessings, dear?" It was an old, old question with them.

"This time I really think we should," Emily Wakefield said seriously.

"Yes," George Wakefield mused as he began to eat. He counted himself a very lucky man. During the war he had been in seven battles without a scratch. Then he had been able to marry Emily, sell out all of their Valdosta property, and move out here to Prospect, arriving at the right time to open the bank. Now he owned the bank, this big eleven-room house, a thousand acres of good grazing land at the upper end of the valley, and held half interest in the Lucky Emily Mine and half interest in the Prospect Mercantile Store. He was not yet a rich man, but he was well on his way.

He swallowed and said to his daughter, "Libby, I want you to help Henry get the stall ready for your new pony this morning. That will be your chore from now on, to keep the stall clean. Henry will show you what to do. Then you can wash up and fetch dinner to me at the bank as usual and we'll eat together." He had to keep her busy while Emily got ready for the party at four o'clock. "You can wait at the bank for your pony and we'll walk home together."

Libby was too thrilled to speak. She knew about the party; in a town where everybody knew everybody else's doings it was impossible to keep a to-do big as a birthday party a secret.

Emily Wakefield said, "I'm afraid the party will be an anticlimax, dear."

"Don't you believe it. Libby will be the envy of every boy and girl present. No more coffee for me, Hazel. Good breakfast as usual, thank you." He pushed his chair back and plucked his watch out of his vest pocket. "I'll be on my way. Beautiful day out."

"We could use some rain. It's so dry." Emily Wakefield couldn't get used to having a little rain during the winter plus a lot of snow and then almost no rain at all the rest of the year.

"I prefer the dryness to the muggy heat of Valdosta. Well, see you at noon, honey. Wipe your mouth and give me a kiss. Not with your hand! Use your napkin." He chuckled. "Oh, well," he sighed, and with a jaunty air he left the room.

Outside on the front porch he set his bowler hat at a distinguished angle and gazed with admiration at the mountains at the north end of the valley. He knew that they were thirty miles away but they looked a lot closer, no more than five miles at most. Back in Georgia a mile was a mile, out here something a mile away looked close enough to touch. Those mountains to the north were the making of the valley, so everybody said; they were high enough to catch enough snow to keep the streams running all year. He went down the steps and stopped in the yard to look at the house. It was still new enough to think about. Emily had wanted to build the house up on a hillside but he didn't like hills for living on. The flatland suited him just fine. Why live on a hill and look down on a valley when you could live in the valley and look up at the hills? Besides, he liked living close to the bank. It was only two blocks away. He could walk it easily in two minutes.

As he opened the gate in the white picket fence that Emily had insisted on, something to remind her of Georgia, he heard Libby calling from the porch. "Bye, Daddy!" He blew her a kiss and strolled on down the street.

The town was growing fast. Already the population was over five hundred. They had a courthouse, two churches, a dozen or more stores, a smelter, several livery stables, and the hope that a railroad would come this way in a year or two. The mines up on the hills to the east of town were producing well with no sign as yet of the ore petering out. He knew of course that the future of the town would be ranches and farms, for mines did have the nasty habit of giving out. Still, it was the mines that had given the town its start. He wondered if he too shouldn't buy some good cows and build a house on the thousand acres. Put a foreman in charge. Later, he decided. He was a banker, not a rancher. He'd hang onto the land; maybe Libby would like a ranch when she grew up. Not likely; she was merely going through a phase of being a tomboy.

"Morning, George."

"Hello, Bill. How goes it? Any badmen around?"

The old marshal grinned. "No more than I can handle. Pretty day, ain't it?"

"The air is like wine. Read that somewhere."

"Wal, don't get drunk on it or I'll throw you in the hoosegow."

George Wakefield chuckled and moved on. He was indeed lucky. He had a host of friends, more than he could count.

"Hello, Doc. Any increase in the population overnight?"

"Not 'less you count a litter of pups, George."

"Only at election time, Doc." He wondered just how many times a man could use the same greetings, day after day, without it getting stale.

At the bank corner he paused and looked around. Everything seemed in good order. Ore wagons. The water wagon wetting down the dust. A pair of—he took a closer look. Prospectors? Indians? One looked like a darky. Both were dressed like Indians. Breechclouts. Apache moccasins. Anyway there were the packed burros, so they must be prospectors. Teedle White was opening his barbershop.

"Morning, Teedle. How's the family?"

"Fit and sassy, George."

"Your boy Jiggs will be at Libby's party this afternoon, won't he, Teedle?"

"Six-shooter and all, George."

George Wakefield laughed dutifully and took another look at the two prospectors as they went into the store. There were a lot of darkies coming West these days. Most of them were good men. He had never owned a slave, didn't believe in it, yet he had fought for the South for four long, miserable years. Strange what a man will fight for. He rapped on the bank's door and Percy Potter let him in.

"Morning, Mr. Wakefield."

"Morning, Percy. Any mice get at the goodies during the night?" He went inside and the teller propped the door back. They were open for business.

Going back to his office, which was at the back of the small lobby, he hung up his hat and coat and opened the big Wells Fargo safe with a brass key. He stood back to let the teller remove his tray; then he took out a stack of ledgers and put them on his desk.

The morning passed with the usual business. The town merchants came in to make deposits and get change. He wrote a letter of credit for Jack Masters, who was taking the eastbound stage, going to St. Louis on a buying trip. Then, along about eleven-thirty the same two prospectors came in. They were wearing new California pants and blue-cotton miner's shirts, and both had visited the barber. The white man looked a lot younger without the whiskers. The darky had been shaved, but his face didn't look much different, only cleaner. They spoke to Percy Potter for a moment; then the teller called out, "Two men to see you about a loan, Mr. Wakefield. Go right on back, gentlemen." Percy Potter was from Vermont.

George Wakefield got up and went around the desk as the two men came into the office. It was his policy to be courteous, even when his first impression warned him that a man would be a bad credit risk. His first impression now was that these two little men would not be good credit risks. Still, he could be wrong, although he didn't miss very often in his summing up of a man.

"Good day, men," he said, holding out his hand to the white man. "Welcome to the town of Prospect. I'm George Wakefield. What can I do for you?" The white man's grip was firm enough, but he appeared nervous. "Have a chair." He motioned toward the one chair and went back around the desk to sit down. He left the black man standing.

The white man looked at the one chair and stayed on his feet. "I'm Kestrel Morgan," he said, taking a position behind the chair. "This is my partner and brother, Snipe Morgan. We need some money to buy us an ore crusher and a dry washer and some blasting powder."

"I see," George Wakefield said. "And where is your mine located, Mr. Morgan?" He spoke to the white man and acted as if the black man was not present. Brother?

"It's out in the desert. South of here. Here's a sample of the ore. It's pretty rich. We worked some up with our arrastra and it ran about two ounces to the ton to our reckoning."

"That's pretty rich ore, all right," the banker freely admitted. He pulled the leather sack towards himself and opened it to reach in and take out a chunk of rose quartz. He opened a desk drawer and took out a magnifying glass. He inspected the quartz and saw fine specks of gold. It was rich ore indeed, far richer than the ore from the Lucky Emily. He emptied the sack on his desk. It was all the same—a lovely sight. He looked at it for a few seconds, then put the magnifying glass back in the drawer and leaned back. "How far out in the desert is your mine?"

"About a hundred miles, more or less."

"Pretty dry out there, isn't it?"

"We've got us a spring near the mine. Not much of a spring as springs go, but enough for us and the girls."

"The girls?"

"Our two burros. They're both jennies. We call them the girls."

"I see. Well, before I can lend you any money, men, I'll have to know something about you." He didn't like turning a man down too quickly. Good manners called for that much. "Tell me something about yourself, Mr. Morgan. Where are you from?"

"We're from Alabama. A place called Elmo; that's south of Mobile about twenty miles or so. My dad had a farm there until a Yankee carpetbagger beat him out of it. He's dead now; so is Mom. That's why we come West, me and Snipe. No sense hanging around after the dog's dead."

"No indeed, Mr. Morgan." The banker looked past the white man at Percy Potter, who was listening as usual. He'd have to put a door up. "Well, er, just how long have you been out here in the West, Mr. Morgan. Very long?"

"About seven years now."

"And you've been prospecting all that time?"

"Not all that time. We were Army scouts down in Arizona Territory for about a year."

"Fighting the Apaches?" Now he began to smell a rodent; these puny-looking men were trying to work a confidence trick on him. He had one or two in the bank on the average of once a week. Army scouts? Hell, they were no bigger than boys.

"Well, not fighting the Apaches. We were scouts, not soldiers. We never killed no Indians."

"But as scouts you sometimes got close to the Apaches, did you not?"

"Well, that was our job. Say, listen, mister. What's all this got to do with lending us some money?"

"Perhaps nothing at all, Mr. Morgan." He liked the show of spunk. "I'm just trying to get to know you well enough to make a decision, that's all. Now, about the mine. How much ore do you figure is in the ledge or vein or whatever it is?"

"How the hell can anybody know that, mister? We only went in a couple of feet. It looks pretty solid back in there though. There's country rock on both sides of the vein. We got out about all we could with a hammer and cold chisel."

The banker leaned forward and picked up a chunk of the quartz. "You said a while ago that your, er, partner is your brother. What did you mean by that? Is he your blood kin or what?"

"No, we didn't have the same dad and mom. Dad bought Snipe's dad fresh off the boat for fifty dollars because he had a broken leg. That was about all Dad could afford to pay for him. Anyway, when the leg healed up and Dad saw how smart old William was, he went up to Mobile and borrowed six hundred dollars on the farm and bought William a wife. Me and Snipe were born the same year, in 1850. Me in June and Snipe in August. So we were brought up together. That's why we're brothers. We've been partners ever since."

"Now I understand," the banker said. "Well, getting back to the loan. I'm afraid your mine is much too far away for me to lend you money on it, Mr. Morgan. I would have to go out there and see it, and take along an expert on mining to make an estimate." He spread his hands.

"Look, mister," the white man said. "Here's the gold we took out of the arrastra." He pulled a poke from his pants pocket and tossed it on the desk. "We spent about half an ounce over in the store for these duds we got on. Not that much. Anyway, that's what we took out of four grindings in the arrastra. With a crusher and a dry washer and some blasting powder and a pound of quicksilver we could pay you back a thousand dollars in no time."

The banker untied the leather thong and poured a little pile of gold dust into his palm. It did look pretty; fine as flour but a shiny yellow. He poured the gold back into the poke and looked up. "I'm afraid I can't help you, men. Why don't you do some prospecting around this area? There's gold all over the mountains and hills. Should you find a good prospect nearby, I'll be glad to have another talk with you."

He consulted his watch and saw that the time was three minutes to twelve. As he looked up, he saw that Libby was coming in the front door with the food hamper. He knew that she would not disturb him while he had clients. Still, he could see no profit in prolonging the talk. "If you'll excuse me, men. You can get coin for your gold from the teller if you'd like. We pay $20.67 the troy ounce and charge two dollars an ounce for impurities and such. There's enough in your poke to buy some blasting powder." He went around the desk, paying no heed to the expressions of disappointment on the men's faces.

"Come on, Snipe," the white man said, and leaving the sample ore on the desk, he took the poke and led the way to the teller's window and slapped the poke down. "Weigh it up, mister."

CHAPTER FIVE

Kestrel was waiting for the old man with the green eyeshade to weigh up the gold when Snipe poked him in the ribs and said in a low voice, "The bandits."

He turned his head as five men came in the door. He recognized the bandit leader at once, and he watched as one man stayed at the door while the others spread out with leveled rifles.

The teller called out, "Robbers, Mr. Wakefield!" Too late. The bandit leader was already at the office doorway.

Kestrel didn't need to be told to raise his hands. He shot them up, and beside him Snipe slowly did the same. Then Kestrel stood fascinated as the bandits went to work. Two men with empty flour sacks rushed into the office past their leader and began filling the sacks from the safe. He saw bags of what could only be gold coins dropped into the sacks. Another bandit went around behind the ironwork teller's cage and began filling another flour sack with money. Into the sack went their poke.

Inside the office the banker had his hands up, and the

little girl in boy's clothes stood in front of him, frozen with astonishment.

Kestrel heard the banker say, "Gower Blount?"

"That's right, George. Never figured you'd see me again, did you?"

"I was told you were dead."

"Not yet, George. Not quite yet." The bewhiskered one looked down at the little girl. "Your kid, eh? What's your name, kid?"

The little girl raised her chin and said, "I don't like you." She didn't sound the least scared.

Blount said, "Ha!" and turned to the two men at the safe. "Get it all, men. Take every penny."

They did, and when all of the sacks had all they could safely hold without bursting one man said, "That's it, boss."

"Good." Blount turned back to the banker. "I'm taking the kid for a hostage, George." The bandit leader's voice was remarkably conversational, so much so that Kestrel thought it might all be a prank. "She'll be all right so long as nobody follows us. But if somebody does follow us, I'll kill the kid the way I just now killed my wife. *My* wife, George." There was menace in the man's low-pitched voice.

Kestrel was watching the banker's face, and he was impressed with the way the man was able to restrain himself. He stood there with his hands raised and said not a word. His face, however, had blanched and his lips were trembling with frustration.

"Ready, boss!"

While Blount kept his rifle leveled, the other four men

slung their rifles over their shoulders and gathered up the sacks. When they were ready, Blount seized the little girl by the arm and jerked her off her feet. "Come along, kid. Come on, dammit!" The little girl struggled, but she wasn't strong enough. She was hauled to the outside door, where Blount stopped. For a moment his eyes lingered on Kestrel, but Kestrel could see that he was not recognized with a clean-shaven face and short haircut and wearing miner's clothes. "So long, George." The man gave a little bow, laughed, and went out the door.

For what seemed to Kestrel a full minute but was only a few seconds he and Snipe, the banker, and the teller stood frozen. Then the banker said in a choked voice, "Go fetch Bill Butterworth, Percy."

The teller snatched off his green eyeshade and darted out the door as hoofbeats sounded outside. A moment later Kestrel heard Snipe mutter with laughter in his voice, "It sure don't take long to get rich, does it? I bet them sacks will weigh a hundred pounds."

Kestrel did some fast, rough figuring and said, "A hundred pounds of gold is worth over twenty-four thousand dollars." He looked at the banker, who seemed in a state of shock. Kestrel started to say something to the man when a whole mob of men came rushing through the door.

During the next minute or two Kestrel was reminded of a flock of chickens with a hawk overhead. Two or three dozen men all trying to talk at once. Nothing got done until an old man wearing the badge of a marshal came in. Suddenly the fussing ceased.

"We'll go with you to catch them rascals, Bill!" one

man volunteered, and he was joined by a chorus of other voices. "We're with you, Bill!" "Tell us what you want done, Bill." "I saw 'em headed south past my place going hell for leather!"

The old marshal ignored them and spoke to the banker. "If they're headed into the desert, we'll catch 'em, George. You all right?"

George Wakefield was still in a daze. He shook his head like a dog with a tick in his ear. "No. No pursuit, Bill. They're got Libby." He dry-washed his face with both hands.

The marshal seemed to sag in his clothes. "That's bad. That ain't good at all." He turned to look over the mob. "Any of you men in the bank when it happened?"

Snipe spoke up. "We were here, marshal. Me and my partner."

"Ever see any of the men before?"

Thinking fast, Snipe said, "Never did, marshal."

Beside him, Kestrel kept quiet.

The marshal turned back to the banker. "I'll have to get up a posse and go after them, George. It's my job."

The banker got a grip on himself. "I'm asking you not to chase them, Bill. I know the leader. Gower Blount. I knew him back in Georgia. Oh, God! He said he killed Emily!" And without further ado he wedged his way through the crowd and shot out the door with half the mob on his heels.

Kestrel knew that Snipe was thinking it wouldn't be much longer and some of the town men would start thinking that they were members of the bandit gang. He looked with faint hope at the counter behind the teller's cage. He'd seen their poke go into a sack, which meant that they had lost their blasting powder money. Except for a few silver coins they'd got in change when they'd bought their new duds, they were flat broke. He noticed that three men had stayed behind and were looking them over. He raised his hands, palms up, and shrugged as he said to Snipe, "Let's go see if we can help." Then he said to the three men, "We'll be around in case the marshal wants to talk to us." And with Snipe beside him he went outside, where more men and women and kids were gathering the way buzzards gather around a dying cow.

Snipe the thinker took over. The natural thing to do was stick around, so they lingered, mixing with the crowd, answering questions. The two partners had known each other so many years that each knew what the other was thinking in any given situation. In their new duds they looked about the same as those around them. The difference was their moccasins, but the high tops were hidden under their pants legs. After a few minutes, when the initial excitement died down to a drone, they moved casually across the street to the watering trough in front of the Prospect Mercantile Store.

There Kestrel hung his hat on the pump and scooped up water from the trough to slosh his face. Snipe did the same, and as they raised up to stand in the hot air and wait for their faces to dry, Kestrel said, "That was some quick thinking, Snipe." They both knew, had they admitted that they had seen the bandits out in the desert five days ago, the marshal would have become suspicious and they would likely be held in Prospect, probably in jail.

Snipe casually looked around. Half the town population had gathered around the bank, but none were close enough to hear them. He said, "Now we know what all the water kegs were for."

Kestrel said, "Yep." He was still trembling from the fright thrown into him inside the bank.

Snipe never trembled, no matter what happened. He said, "They got an awful lot of gold."

"Yep," was all Kestrel could manage.

"They got our poke too."

"Yep."

"They also got just about what we need plus a little bonus."

"Yep."

"That banker won't let the marshal follow them bandits."

"Nope."

"There's no reason why we can't though."

A brief pause, then Kestrel said, "Nope."

A man came hurrying down the street from the west, waving his hands and calling out, "They killed Emily Wakefield! They killed the hired girl and the hired hand too!"

Like a stampeding herd, the crowd took off down the street, chasing the informer, who had spun around to avoid being trampled.

Snipe said, "Let's tag along. It'll look odd if we don't."

So they put on their hats and followed the crowd. They didn't get a look at the bodies. They didn't want to. It was enough to learn that the bandits actually had murdered three people. They mingled with the crowd outside a white picket fence and admired the elegance of the big white house where the banker lived. To avoid suspicion, they stayed at the back of the crowd, yet they were still a part of it, seemingly as curious as anyone else.

After a while the marshal stepped out of the house onto the front porch and raised his hands to silence the crowd. "Now listen to me!" he said in a loud voice. "You all know that some robbers held up the bank. Well, they also killed Mrs. Wakefield and Hazel Mann and Henry Dobbs." A savage grumble swept through the crowd. There were at least two hundred people present, men and women and a lot of children. "All right. Calm down now." The noise slowly died away.

"The robbers also took Libby Wakefield along with them as a hostage. The leader of the gang's name is Gower Blount. Mr. Wakefield recognized him; knew him back in Georgia. I've got a good description, so I'm going to send telegraphs to every marshal and sheriff and army post around the country. Now listen to me. I don't want anybody going after them robbers. You hear that? Nobody! Blount has threatened to kill the little girl if anybody shows up on their tails. Is that clear?"

The crowd didn't like it, and the old marshal seemed to sense the mood, so he put some of them to work. "I need fifty good men to spread out south of town to make sure nobody takes a notion to go robber hunting. Deputy's pay of two dollars a day. You men with guns step up here on the porch."

"That deals us out," Snipe muttered as at least eighty armed men climbed up on the porch.

"All right. That's enough. Now the rest of you go about your business."

Slowly and reluctantly the crowd began to drift away,

and the partners drifted along back towards the center of town. The midday sun was blazing down from a clear sky, so most of the people began looking for some shade.

As they passed the bank, headed east, Kestrel casually looked around to see if anybody was close enough to hear, and said, "How do you figure to go about it, Snipe?"

"Nine men," Snipe mused. "It won't be easy to do."

"No, it won't. And we just might get a hunk of lead in our briskets."

"No, that won't happen. Don't even think about that. Think about all that gold. How do you feel about taking the banker's gold, Kes?"

"I sure won't miss any sleep over it. Not after the way he treated us. Especially you. The bastard must think he's still back in Georgia. What about the little girl? That mean old coyote won't hesitate to kill her if we show up and give him some trouble."

"We'll take the little girl away from him first."

"How?"

"I'll find a way. The important thing right now is to decide whether we go after that gold. You game?"

"Well, I don't hanker to get shot. But yes, I'm game."

"That's it then. Let's go on down to the stable and get the girls. We'll head east out of town a ways and then look for some shade to wait for sunset. Then we'll slip through the picket line. It'll be pretty thin by sundown. Those men won't like standing out there in the sun doing nothing."

When they entered the livery barn, a boy of about twelve already taller than they were jumped on the partners like a bobcat on a rabbit. "Hey! You hear about the bank being robbed?"

"Is that a fact?" Snipe said.

"Yeah. They made off with a million dollars. Hey, you gonna be here for a spell? I wanta go see. Don't tell my dad where I went though." And before Snipe could respond, the boy was gone. That was a piece of good luck that they hadn't counted on.

Snipe quickly went through to the corral in back to get the burros while Kestrel gathered the empty water gourds to fill at the pump. He didn't like taking drinking water from a well so near a stable but he figured that a well in this area would have to be a hundred feet deep or deeper, so he took the chance. When Snipe had the packsaddles on the burros and everything loaded aboard except the water gourds, he joined Kestrel to work the pump handle. The pump gave a good flow, so Kestrel was able to hold the necks of four gourds under the spout at the same time. They worked fast, but they tried not to give any show of haste. They both realized that it wouldn't take the town marshal much longer to realize that the two men wearing new duds inside the bank at the time of the robbery just might be in cahoots with the bandits.

Twenty minutes after they had entered the barn, they were ready to leave. They looked at each other, nodded their heads, and each took a lead rope and walked slowly out the front entrance.

They had gone only a few steps when Snipe said, "Hold up." He handed Kestrel the lead rope of his burro and went back inside, digging in his pocket for a fifty-cent piece as he went. He found the dust-filled office on one side and went in. Looking around, he found a nickel writing tablet and a pencil stub. On one page he printed in large letters: 50¢ PAY FOR TWO BURROS—MUCH OBLIGE. The beanpole boy would probably find the coin and filch it, not bothering to tell his dad. Turning to leave again, Snipe paused and turned back. He added to the note: TOOK PENCIL AND TABLET—DIME MORE. He pocketed the pencil and tucked the tablet under his belt and hid it with his shirttail.

As Kestrel could have told anybody who cared to know, this was typical of Snipe Morgan. The Bushman planned ahead, often months ahead. He was not infallible; he sometimes made mistakes, but they were more often than not of little consequence.

Snipe was thinking that one day soon he would have to talk to the bandits. He wouldn't be able to get close enough to talk without getting shot, so with the pencil and tablet he could write them a message.

As he was going outside, the stable owner walked up. At once Snipe said, "Hello there. I left four bits in your tack room along with a dime for your pencil stub and writing tablet. Hope that's enough."

"Suits me, boy. Where you headed?"

"We figured we'd try our luck around the other side of that hill where all the mines are."

"You won't find much ground that ain't already staked out. Hear about the bank robbery?" The man was well over six feet tall and Snipe guessed that he wouldn't weigh much over a hundred pounds. He certainly couldn't deny his son.

"We not only heard, we were there." Snipe figured the truth was called for just in case the man had seen him or Kestrel in the crowd. "How much money you reckon they got?"

"All there was. They got three hundred of my own money too." The man looked back the way he'd come. "Well, so long, boy," and he got in out of the sun.

East of the town, houses extended out for a good mile. They had to go another mile before coming to a dry wash that came down from the hill where the mines were located. The wash was flanked by twin rows of cottonwood trees. Snipe chose to go off the road on the left side rather than the right. It was a small thing, but it could prove important. Were they to camp on the south side, it would look as if they were planning to head south into the desert. If they camped on the north side of the stage road, whoever saw them might think they were headed northeast around the hill. For the same reason, he chose to camp in the shade of a cottonwood within sight of the road. They were not trying to hide.

"We'll catch some sleep now, Kes. Then we'll eat before sundown and be on our way. We'll have to travel fast to get ahead of them bandits."

"Ahead?" Kestrel asked as he began unloading one of the burros.

"That's right. We're going to deprive the bastards of their water. After we take the little girl away from them."

"I want to live long enough to see just how you go about doing that little chore," Kestrel said. "Not that I doubt you can do it. You hungry now?"

"Nope. Let's sleep first. We'll be on the go hard all night."

"Well, it's already late, so I'll just put on a pot of beans." And he went around gathering wood while Snipe stretched out in the shade and went to sleep.

CHAPTER SIX

The sun was an inch high in the west when they crossed the stage road and headed south down the dry wash. Snipe had looped a half hitch around the muzzle of the first burro and held a short leash the better to urge the little beast along at a fast pace. The second burro, its leash rope made fast to the first burro's packsaddle, followed along at a distance of about seven feet. The long leash rope was to allow the second burro a chance to see where it was stepping. Kestrel was behind the second burro about ten feet, a distance that gave him a chance to see where he was putting his feet.

A burro's natural pace is a dancing trot that is almost a run, and tonight Snipe intended to move at that pace or faster. So, for the first hundred yards or so he kept tugging at the leash until the burros were going at their fastest walking pace, a pace that would average about four miles every hour.

The Papago Indians' saguaro-harvest moon was approaching full and had risen an hour before sunset. Already it was helping to light up the cottonwood trees that were fast petering out as the dry wash widened to spread out over the flat desert. The cottonwood tree is a water hog, so it cannot live except in places where there is sufficient ground water below the surface.

In the gathering dusk, Snipe spotted a town man sitting on the west bank of the wash near the last cottonwood a quarter or so from the stage road. He kept going, much as if he had not seen the man, and he was a good ten yards past him when the man raised up and called out, "Hold up there!"

Snipe kept going, maintaining the same pace, and Kestrel, as he passed the man, saw he was drawing a pistol from his belt. "Marshal Bill sent us!" He called and kept going. Ten yards farther on he looked back over his right shoulder and saw the man taking aim at the sky. A moment after the warning shot they were out of range. The ruse had worked well enough to get the job done. Kestrel did not relish being shot at, even with a pistol at long range.

The town man rushed back to Prospect to inform the marshal.

The wash petered out and became desert pavement, with wide and evenly spaced creosote bushes. The landscape was moonwashed now, and Snipe with his good night vision could see with ease. Placing the moon over his left shoulder, he set his course and settled down to a steady lope that matched the pace of the burros.

Kestrel, bringing up the rear, kept thinking about the bandits. While eating supper, they had talked. It was Snipe's guess that the bandits would travel fairly fast for some twenty miles or so then slow down to save the horses. Kestrel was somewhat amazed that the tough little mustangs had made it across the desert at all while traveling by daylight. He suspected that the horses by now were close to being crippled. He had not seen any leg wrappings on the horses five days ago that would have indicated that the bandits knew enough to do just that, wrap the legs and keep the wrappings moist to keep the legs and hoofs cool. He further suspected that none of the bandits was a desert man. He could not remember seeing even one indication that any of the bandits knew how to travel safely in the desert in the dead of summer.

The desert air was beginning to cool now. In another few hours it would actually be chilly.

Kestrel continued to ponder about the bandits. They were nine to their two. They were armed with excellent repeating rifles and pistols to their one bow and three spears. One mistake and both he and Snipe would be dead. Was it worth it?

Snipe seemed to think it was.

The alternative was to return to the mine, work ore to get a hundred dollars worth of gold, use that to buy blasting powder and a pound of quicksilver, work more ore until they got enough money to buy a crusher and dry washer, then go on working the mine until they could take out a hundred pounds of gold. That would take all of five years, to his way of thinking. Meanwhile besting the bandits and taking the banker's gold shouldn't take more than ten days or so.

Would it pay them to buy a dry washer before they bought the crusher? That would certainly save a lot of time and work winnowing the arrastra-pulverized ore by hand. Could they make a dry washer the way they had made about everything else? No, they'd tried making a dry washer. Nothing worked.

Snipe came to a sudden halt up ahead and Kestrel kept going. He bumped into the second burro and said, "Beg pardon, girl."

"Water stop, Kes."

"Have we traveled five miles already?"

"Close to it."

Kestrel looked around. This was wide-open desert, one of the countless areas where the ground was too rocky to sustain even the hardy desert plants. There was no more desolate place on earth. Bathed in moonlight, with a million stars shining down and the Milky Way a bright swathe across the sky, he got a feeling of insignificance so intense it made him shiver.

"You all right, Kes?"

"What? Oh, yes, I'm all right." He dug out the big pot and a half-dozen water gourds and let the burros drink their fill. He drank a gourdful himself and so did Snipe.

"How are your moccasin soles holding up?"

"All right. I think I've lost two or three layers is all. What about yours?" Their moccasins each had started off new with ten layers of antelope hide for the soles. Whenever they wore out four layers, they cemented on more layers. They always brought along leather for that, with a small gourd full of piñon pitch for glue. A barefooted man in the desert couldn't travel a hundred feet.

"You're being awful quiet, Kes. Having second thoughts about tackling the bandits?"

"Not second thoughts. I'm still working on my first thoughts. Do you realize that one mistake and we'll be dead? One little mistake."

Snipe squatted down in a position Kestrel remembered old William assuming when out in the Alabama woods and tipped up his water gourd. When he lowered the gourd, he said, "We can give up the notion if you say so."

Kestrel sat down on the rocky ground and crossed his legs. The air was quite cool now, and off in the distance a pair of coyotes were serenading them. After a long silence he said, "No. Let's go on. Somebody's got to do something for that little girl."

"She'll die if we don't, Kes. That man Blount has no intention about letting her go free. You heard the banker say he knew Blount back in Georgia. That means the robbery and the killings were for revenge. He won't hesitate a second about killing the girl."

"I know that. But if we take the gold, how will we get the little girl back to her daddy and not have her tell him we've got his money?"

"She won't know we've got the money. Not if my plan works out."

"Do you intend to kill those nine men?"

"You asked me that before, Kes. The answer is still not unless I have to. And I don't think I'll have to."

"Well"—and Kestrel got to his feet—"you know what you're doing. You always do. And you know I'll go along and do what I can." What he was trying to say was that he was not a brave man, not as brave as Snipe, anyway. "Now a thought," he went on. "Bright as the moonlight is, don't you think them bandits will get the idea to travel at night and lay up during daylight?"

"I've thought about that. They might, but somehow I don't think they will. A man on horseback, even in moonlight, has a difficult time following hoofprints out on this hardbaked desert. They're retracing the tracks they made going north. They have to if they want to find their buried water kegs."

"A man on foot could lead them at night," Kestrel pointed out.

"True. They may even think of that too. We'll know by tomorrow night when we cross their trail if they're ahead of us. I'm banking on them traveling a lot slower than we'll travel. Anyway, one more night after tonight is all we need. We'll take the girl, and after that they can travel night or day. It won't make any difference then. Ready for another five miles?"

"After we have some syrup." Kestrel dug out one of the saguaro shoes filled with syrup, pried off the clay lid, and poured a mugful for Snipe. He refilled the mug for himself, drank it, and emptied the shoe into two of the empty water gourds. He tossed aside the shoe.

They continued on at the same fast pace. The rocky terrain changed to gently rolling hills covered with small creosote bushes and bur sage, which changed to a dense forest of cholla cactus. Snipe slowed the pace because of the many cholla joints that had fallen from the parent plants and literally covered the ground. They wove their way along, gathering cholla joints that stuck to their moccasins. When the cholla forest thinned out, they stopped and helped each other rid their moccasins and leggins of the cholla joints by using two creosote sticks together like a pair of scissors, flicking the fist-size joints away. Any effort to try picking them off would be a greenhorn's trick.

The moon reached its zenith and began its descent. They stopped every hour or so to drink water and saguaro syrup and chew on jerky. The miles unrolled behind them, and when daylight came they had covered over thirty miles. Still they went on, for speed was essential, stopping only when the sun began to heat the desert floor enough for them to feel heat through the soles of their moccasins. They took shelter in the shade of a clump of organpipe cactus alongside a dry wash that came down from a black hill of volcano rock. As far as they could see in all directions, there was nothing but numerous such volcanic hills brooding like sleeping black giants.

While Kestrel unloaded the burros and started a cooking fire, Snipe took one of the spears and the throwing stick and went in search of meat. He returned with a young jackrabbit and a four-foot-long bull snake. These Kestrel roasted and after they had eaten they settled down to wait out the sun.

Before sundown they ate tepary beans and rabbit stew with tortillas and syrup and loaded the burros to continue. Two hours later Snipe changed course toward the southwest and slowed down, watching the ground for the tracks of the bandits. After a while he had Kestrel come forward to lead the burros while he went on ahead about fifty feet; when he came upon the tracks, he didn't want any burro tracks nearby.

The full moon was nearing its zenith when Snipe called

back to Kestrel to stop. He went back and said, "I found the tracks. Now we have to slow down. We're ahead of them. The hoofprints go only the one way, toward the north."

Kestrel said, "We must be a good forty miles from Prospect."

"All of that much," Snipe agreed. "My guess is we're no more than five miles ahead of them. That providing their horses are still sound." He faced the north and looked and listened. He could hear only the night sounds of the desert—the yipping of coyotes, the scurry of numerous small animals. He heard the cry of a rabbit, taken by desert fox or coyote or owl. The night was alive with the sounds of many creatures that are almost never seen after the sun comes up. The area was one of widely spaced creosote bushes with bur sage dotting the ground in between, and here and there an occasional yucca and a sprinkling of barrel cactus. The barrel cactus all leaned toward the southwest, the desert compass.

Snipe said, "Now I want you to draw back about fifty feet, Kes. Then head south. I'll follow the tracks and call out for you to go to the right or left according to how the tracks go. In any case try to keep the burros away from the tracks. I'll go along slow. We've got plenty of moonlight left before daylight. What we're looking for now is one of their camping sites. And their buried water kegs. If my guess is right, we'll find the next campsite about twenty miles farther on, give or take five miles. How are you holding up?"

"I'm all right."

"Good. Let's go on then." Snipe went back to the tracks

and turned left. He was satisfied that Kestrel would not say he was all right if he was not. Too much depended on their being honest with each other to tell a fib about not being tired when they were.

Mourning doves were calling to each other and the sun was poking its head up above a naked hill of black volcano rock to their left when Snipe saw a white rag tied to a tall paloverde tree and came upon the remains of a campfire near a narrow wash that ran east to west. The doves told him that there was water somewhere within ten to twenty miles in one direction or another because he knew from years of observation that doves must have water at least twice a day, usually flying off to the watering place shortly after daylight and again before sunset.

He called to Kestrel to stop while he looked around. He stood in one spot to avoid making too many moccasin prints and studied the site. The wash was lined with mesquite and paloverde, with patches of prickly-pear cactus and clumps of dry-looking brittlebush scattered in between. The ground was sandy and showed signs of many boots prints and the prints of horses and mules.

He picked the most likely spot for burying water kegs and eased himself around to it. Down on his knees, he dug down with his hands and soon struck a wooden keg. More digging and he counted four kegs. Satisfied, he recovered the kegs and eased back and away from the site to cut a branch from a paloverde tree. He used the branch as a broom to obliterate his moccasin tracks and walked backwards to where Kestrel was waiting, brushing out his tracks behind him.

Krestrel laughed when he saw Snipe backing up towards him. "I think you're giving those bandits more credit for smartness than they deserve, old buddy. I don't think they could tell a boot track from a moccasin track or a deer's hind hoof from a burro's."

"Maybe so, Kes, but we're not sure about that." Snipe turned around. "Four water kegs buried." He looked past Kestrel's head at the black hill some two hundred yards away to the east. "That's a good spot up there to hide and watch them when they get here. Take the girls back the way you came and circle north around the hill to the other side. We'll make camp there and late this coming afternoon we'll find a spot up there on the hill. I'll blot out the burro tracks behind you."

Kestrel grinned and turned the burros around. He supposed that he and Snipe were both alive and doing well simply because Snipe didn't take unnecessary risks.

A half hour later, as the sun was beginning to bear down with fierce intensity and the cool of the night traded places with the heat of the day, they were camped in the shade of a ten-foot-tall ironwood tree on the eastern side of the black hill.

They ate corn-flour flapjacks with saguaro syrup and drank joint-fir tea and stretched out in the shade to get some much-needed rest and sleep.

When they were awakened just before midday by the sun shining on them, they moved around to the east side of the shade tree and Snipe used the pencil stub and writing tablet to draw a map of the bandit's campsite from memory. He outlined how they would take the little girl.

"The campsite is here, on the north side of a narrow wash that runs east to west. The bandits will sleep on the west side of the paloverde right about here. I know that because they slept there the last time and people are creatures of habit. The moon comes up about an hour after sunset, so there won't be any real darkness. We'll come down from the hill at moonrise and go down the wash to within about fifty feet of the paloverde. You station yourself at that spot with one of the spears.

"I intend to sneak on down the wash, using the bank for cover, then crawl in among them to find the girl. When I find her I'll snatch her up fast and run back up the wash past you. If anybody follows right away, use the spear on him. If nobody follows right away, you leave and follow me. We'll circle back around the hill to here and then take off running to get away from any pursuit."

"What if there's a sentry?"

"If there is, I'm hoping he'll be asleep. But I don't think there'll be a sentry. Those bandits are not soldiers and they'll be pretty tired. They go to sleep soon after dark is my guess, providing nobody has chased them from Prospect, which again I doubt. If there is a sentry and he's awake, I'll just have to knock him out with a rock before I take the girl."

Kestrel continued to play the role of devil's advocate, a role he had played many times before. "The girl will scream her head off when you snatch her awake."

"That I expect. But I intend to get away so fast the bandits won't have time to react before I'm gone."

Kestrel considered the plan for a while. He wasn't eager to get at it, but he couldn't see anything basically wrong with it. It was daring, and barring unforeseen happenings, it should work. If anybody could do the trick, Snipe Morgan could.

He nodded his agreement and Snipe said, "We'll load the girls and leave them here tied up and go around to get settled on the hillside about two hours before sunset. It'll be too hot up there on the west side of the hill with the sun beating down on it to go any sooner. Even if the bandits are already there, we can sneak up the hill without them seeing us. The only chancy part is if they see us climbing the hill while they're approaching the campsite. We can be careful about that. Now I think we should get some grub ready and eat, because we won't have time later on." He took a spear and went hunting, to return in less than a minute with a twenty-pound desert tortoise he'd found under the crusty ledge of a caliche.

"Well, fry me for a catfish!" Kestrel crowed when he saw the tortoise. "That's the best bygod eating the desert can provide." He built a big fire with dead cactus wood, which gave off no smoke at all, and after killing the tortoise with his knife, he laid it on the fire whole to roast in the shell. An hour later they sat down to a feast.

CHAPTER SEVEN

She had got over being scared. Now she was looking for a chance to run away from these nasty old badmen. If only her ankles weren't tied to the stirrups on both sides of this old mule, she'd jump off and run over and hide behind that old cactus tree. She wondered when her daddy would come and beat up all these old men and take her home. He didn't come last night. She'd tried to stay awake for him. Tonight he'd come for sure.

Sure is hot. Can't swallow anymore. She'd die first before she'd ask one of these old badmen for a drink. Smelly old men. She'd bet they never took a bath. She stared ahead at the back of the nasty old man with the whiskers. He was the worst of the lot. She looked back at the rest of the badmen, strung out behind her like ants coming away from a dead bug. She saw the boy called Joe Brown smile at her, but she'd die before she'd smile back. Poor white trash, that's what Mama would call them.

She looked ahead again at the shimmering haze. A roadrunner bird scampered along ahead for a while; crazy old bird. She wished she had her pony; she could run away then. Dadblame but it's hot. She rubbed her dry face and wished she had her hat. Dang thing fell off. She saw Joe Brown riding up beside her.

"Want another drink, honey?" He was holding out a canteen for her to take. She ignored him, looking straight ahead. "Take the damn water, girl!" he snapped at her.

"I don't want it. Leave me alone!"

In his saddle, Joe Brown was two feet taller than she was, riding on the mule. So he moved his horse closer and turned the canteen bottom up, spilling water on her head.

When the water hit her, she couldn't help crying, "Oooooo!" From frying-pan hot one second to near freezing the next. She felt icy all over. Then she felt marvelously cool.

"Next time don't be so damn stubborn, you little snip," Joe said, and added, still holding out the canteen, "Now drink."

She took the canteen and drank. When she handed it back, she said, "Thank you. But I still don't like you. Not one bit."

Joe shrugged his shoulders and said, "Who cares?" He tugged on his reins and pulled his horse back.

The wetness didn't last long. About two minutes, she guessed. Then she was just about as hot as ever.

A while later the old man they called Stump came riding up to the smelly old man with the whiskers and hair growing out of his nostrils and rode alongside. She could hear him say, "Nobody back there, boss. If there is, they're holding a long way back. Sure is bygod hot, ain't it?"

Blount said, "They can't tote enough water to catch up with us."

"Well, I gotta say you figured it out mighty clever, boss. When you figure to share out the loot?"

"Not before we get to Yucca Flat."

"Well now, the men don't think that's fair, boss. They figure you ought to share out right now, just in case like."

"And what do you figure, old man?"

"Well, I figure it'll feel mighty good having my share in my saddlebags. Toting it all on that mule with the girl sort of gives me the jitters like."

They rode on in silence for a spell and then Blount said, "Okay, Stump. Ride back and tell them we'll share out when we make camp. And send Magpie back a mile or two. Oh, and tell Hobart to ride up here."

"Sure thing, boss."

Libby said to herself as the old man wheeled his horse around and rode past her going back, They think I'm too little to understand what they're saying.

A whole covey of black hills came into view up ahead. She didn't know how far away they were, but they looked as close as the mountains north of home looked so she guessed about thirty miles. She kept watching the hills all afternoon and they didn't seem to get any closer, not even close enough to spit on, as she'd heard Henry the hired man say lots of times about the mountains north of home.

Twice more Joe rode up and gave her his canteen, and she didn't make any fuss about it. She liked him a little better, but not very much. Once he pointed out some buzzards soaring way up overhead and said, "If you don't drink up, them buzzards will come down and gobble you up, girl."

She watched the buzzards, circling, circling, and never once did she see one flap its wings.

For a while after she drank the delicious water, she found herself interested in things they passed. A flicker bird perched inside a hole high up in a tall saguaro. Another time she saw a long black snake in a cholla cactus tree and wondered if the cactus spines ever hurt the snake. She saw more jackrabbits than she could count, one hunkered in the shade of every bush it seemed, not hopping out unless the horses got too close.

The man called Hobart came up to ride alongside Gower Blount, but they talked so low she couldn't make out what they were saying. Whisperers are always up to mischief, she'd heard Mama say.

Her skin was hot and dry and she was having dizzy spells when a halt was called about an hour before sundown. Off to the left was a hill, one of the hills she'd been watching all afternoon. There were other hills all around. Joe untied her ankles as the others were coming up. He lifted her down and set her in the shade of a big paloverde tree where it was cool. Blount had taken her boots and had them in his saddlebag to keep her from running away.

Looking up, she saw a white rag tied to a branch and guessed it was a sign of some sort. Two of the men used short-handled shovels to dig up four water kegs, the same as they'd done the evening before. The horses and the mule were given a washbasin full of water each, and the men filled their canteens.

"This here keg done went and sprung a leak," she heard one man say.

She didn't hear the bewhiskered one respond. She saw that he was busy unloading the mule she'd been riding on —the flour sacks full of her father's money.

Joe gave her a canteen full of water and left her to help cook supper. She was so worn out and sick to her stomach she fell asleep.

When she awoke it was almost dark and Joe was standing over her holding a blue enamel plate. "Here you are, honey. Beans and fried ham and some skillet bread. Fix you right up."

When she tried to sit up, she discovered that her ankles were tied together the same way they had been the evening before. She was helped up to a sitting position. She took the plate of food and said, "Thank you."

"You're welcome, honey," Joe said, and went back around the tree where the others were fussing among themselves. She listened while she ate.

"What I'm saying is them mustangs're going lame on us. Ain't that so, Moss?"

"That's right, boss. It's the heat doing it. The ground's too hot. Heats up their hoofs and the heat climbs up the legs and cooks their legbones. I heard tell it could do that but I never believed it till now."

The man called Magpie said, "There's a way to fix that. Leastways keep it from getting any worser. You wraps you some rags around their legs and you pour water on them wrappings."

"We ain't got no water to spare for that. Hardly got enough to put in their bellies."

It was Joe who said, "Heck, we're having a full moon these nights. Why don't we travel at night and lay up during the day."

There followed a minute of silence, as if everyone present felt stupid for not having thought of that days ago.

Then Blount said, "If we travel at night we'll lose the trail."

Joe wouldn't let him save face. "What about one of us going ahead on foot. You sure can't miss the trail that close to it."

Another minute of silence.

"When is moon-up tonight?" Blount asked.

"Right about sunset; maybe a little after." Joe was a moon-watcher.

Blount made the decision. "All right. We'll let the horses forage for three, maybe four hours, then we go on the way Joe said."

Libby sopped the plate clean with a hunk of the skillet bread, and a minute later Gower Blount came around the tree to get her. He dragged her by her arm to where his saddle was on the ground and told her to lie down. When she did, he tied another rope around her legs and made the end fast to a nearby creosote bush. He didn't say anything.

She lay on her back and gazed up at the heaven that was beginning to show stars. Tonight she was positively sure Daddy would come for her. All she had to do was stay awake. He would come when the bandits were all asleep and cut the rope with his pocketknife and take her away.

CHAPTER EIGHT

The two desert men were roasting behind an upjut of volcanic rock on the bare hillside when Snipe said, "Here they come."

The glare of the westering sun was intense. Kestrel shaded his eyes, desert-style, from the glare reflected off the desert floor by grabbing his nose with a fist. With his hat brim pulled down to his eyebrows and his fist gripping his nose, the total glare from the sky and the desert floor was reduced almost by half. He peered to the north through scrinched eyelids.

They had arrived on the hill minutes before, and already he had drunk one gourd empty and was well along on another. A full minute passed before Kestrel spotted movement about three miles away. He shifted his eyes toward the campsite and saw a redtailed hawk perched atop the paloverde that held the white rag.

As he watched, a tarantula wasp buzzed in to alight on his upraised fist. He brushed it away and Snipe said, "No movements, Kes. They can see this hill as good as we can see them."

"Sorry. Stopped thinking for a second. You know something, Snipe. Here we are squatting up here roasting half to death and for some reason I can't put my finger on I still like the desert. Something about the desert that gets to a man after a few years."

Snipe turned his head slowly and looked at him. "I bet it got to them horses. Look how droopy the head is on that lead horse."

Kestrel stared hard. "Hell, from here I can't tell a horse from a mule. You know I don't have eyesight good as yours."

"Maybe you need a pair of them specs."

"Naw, it ain't that. I reckon I see as good as any white man. You must be half hawk."

"Or buzzard?"

Kestrel wet his finger with spit and rubbed it on his eyelids. It helped his vision for a few seconds, long enough to see the droopy-headed horse. "I'd bet on you against a buzzard any day, partner. Is that the little girl on the second horse?"

"Yep. Only she's on a mule. Got her legs tied to the stirrups. She's droopy-headed too."

"Poor kid."

"Yeah, poor kid. I been thinking, Kes. I bet that banker would lend us all the money we need when we take his kid back to him."

"That he will," Kestrel said. "How the devil are we going to get her back to her dad anyway? You think about that any? If we take her back, we'll have to take the money back too."

Snipe frowned. "I'm not about to take that gold back to no banker. We'll see that he gets his kid back, somehow.

But that gold I'm going to bygod keep. My share of it anyway."

"If he asks us about the money, we'll tell him it's an even swap. The kid for the money. How's that sound?"

"There ain't no kid no-place worth no twenty-odd thousand dollars, Kestrel Morgan. Shoot, you know how much your daddy paid for my dad. Fifty measly old dollars. Take that back. Fifty dollars ain't so measly. Wasn't back then anyway. From what your daddy used to tell us how hard a dollar was to come by."

"Your daddy was worth more than any fifty dollars, Snipe Morgan, and you well know it. If he hadn't been crippled up like he was, I bet he would of fetched five, maybe six hundred. Heck, your mom cost six hundred. Worth every penny of it, too. Took Pop twelve years to pay off that mortgage. Longer. We were both eleven years old at the time. Remember the big feast we had?"

"I remember," Snipe said. He was silent for a minute, watching the approaching horsemen. "How much you reckon that little girl will weigh?"

"Oh, sixty, maybe seventy pounds. Why?"

"I was just thinking about toting her and doing some all-out running at the same time."

"Oh." Kestrel hadn't thought about that.

"We'd better duck our heads now, Kes. They'll be looking up here for the next little while. Natural thing to do. Once they settle down they won't be so alert."

They sat with their backs to the upjut of rock. Kestrel thought about the tasty tortoise meat they'd eaten. They'd eaten a lot of strange creatures since they'd been living in the desert. Snakes of all kinds, lizards, bobcat, deer, antelope, lynx cat, coyote, tortoise, cottontail and jackrabbits, quail, now and then a wild turkey when they went into the high mountains, roadrunners, ground squirrels, prickly-pear pads and fruit, fishhook cactus, sego lily bulbs, mesquite beans—the list was almost endless. Once they'd eaten a big hoot owl. Javalina pig. That was good eating, wild pig. Dangerous to fool with though. It wasn't a bad life at all, living in the desert.

"You know, Snipe. I don't know if I want to go back to Alabama after all. What would I go back for? Dad and Mom both dead. Mary Lee's married and I don't like her husband even a little bit. Sure do miss your daddy though. Now there was a real good man. He sure did learn us a lot, didn't he?"

Snipe turned his palm up and waved his hand from side to side. "This is Papa's kind of place, Kes. He lived in a desert over in Africa. Very much like this one here to hear him tell about it. I bet he sure would have liked living here with us." Snipe's dad had been dead for nine years.

Kestrel whistled through his front teeth. "That sure would be something. You and me and your dad. Remember the bows and arrows he made for us when we were about eight? He never did find a plant to make poison with. Anyway, I never did learn to shoot a bow so's I could hit a barn with it. You sure can though. Remember the squirrels you used to hit with your arrows down in the branch behind the big sawdust pile?"

All of this talk they had talked many times before. They were very much like an old married couple, sitting on the porch in rockers, saying nothing, all talked out years ago. It was the circumstances that was making them talk old subjects now.

Snipe nodded. "I was pretty good. Not near so good as Dad was. Ducks on the wing. I never could do that."

"You can too. You just ain't tried lately, that's all. Nobody can sneak up on an antelope the way you can, old buddy. Close enough to down him with a spear. That's close."

"I've got me some sneaking up to do coming up pretty soon now. I wonder if that boss bandit is smart enough to put out a sentry and make him stay awake. You reckon he is?"

"Hard to say. I know I bygod would, what with all that gold in his poke." Kestrel twacked his tongue. "Still, I bet you take that little girl even if there's two or three sentries awake. Bet you a whole nickel you do."

"I sure am hoping she don't cry out too soon." He cocked his head to one side so the water gourd wouldn't show above his head and tilted it, letting the cool water gurgle down his throat. "Have some."

"Don't mind if I do."

After a while the sun set and twilight fell. Snipe turned around slowly and eased his head above the rock. In the gathering dusk he peered down at the camp, and after a while he said, "I can see the little girl. She's this side of the paloverde, laying down. Her legs are tied together. The horses and the one mule are hobbled. Wonder what they did with the other mules. Turned them loose most likely. Them nags down there look too dang tired to eat. I can see the bandits all in a group on the other side of the tree. Looks like they're dividing up the loot. Ease your head up and take a look."

Kestrel raised up, slow and easy.

"See the saddles on the ground the other side of the men?" Snipe pointed out. "That's where they slept the last time." He sniffed. "Blessed if I don't smell fried ham. Smell it?"

Kestrel sniffed. "Nope. All I smell is hot creosote bush."

"Well, I can," Snipe said and licked his lips. "Good old home-smoked ham. Been a long time since we had any good ham. Can't remember the last time I ate a big slab of smoked ham with redeye gravy on a pile of grits."

"Hush before I bite your head off."

Snipe chuckled. "That's something to go back to Alabama for, old buddy. Fried ham and redeye gravy."

"That is just about enough to get me back there, all right enough."

"Come on down to Mexico with me, why don't you. Ride around us a big ranch and make eyes at them black-eyed women." Snipe's voice lowered to a whisper. "That sure would be something. You and me on us a big spread." He started to stand up when Kestrel touched his arm.

"Snipe. You know you and your daddy and mom were never slaves. You know that, don't you?"

"I know it, Kes. You ready?"

"Yes. And you take care, you hear."

"I'll take care."

That was as close as they had ever come to showing overt affection for each other. The soft purple glow of twilight was fading and the stars were beginning to show as Snipe led the way down the slope of the hill.

They had changed their store-bought clothes for their usual garb and they looked like a couple of Indians, one black with short peppercorn hair and one burnt a dark brown by the sun with short-cropped brown hair. One wore an Indian headband; one a floppy-brimmed antelope-hide hat. Both had sheath knives; one carried a seven-foot spear with a throwing stick.

The desert night creatures were beginning to stir; they heard the twit-twit of an elf owl, and all around the hills coyotes were having a bash. The doves that had been calling to each other, sounding so very much like owls, were settling down for the night. There was a slight breeze out of the west. It was the time of evening when sounds carried a long way. They could hear the bandits talking among themselves, their words alternately clear and muddled.

They were both conscious of the fact that rattlesnakes that spend the daylight hours in underground dens come out after sunset to do their hunting, and rattlesnakes on the hunt will rarely give prior warning before striking. It was a hazard they would have to put up with. Kangaroo rats and pack rats scurried out of their path as they went silently down the narrow wash.

Some fifty feet from the bandits, they both settled down to become dark blurs like the bushes along the banks. They could hear the bandits clearly now; they were talking about traveling at night. Then they heard the bandit leader say that they would rest for a while and then go on. Another piece of good luck.

With a whispered "Stay here" to Kestrel, Snipe got down on his belly, and staying close to the north bank of the wash, he slithered along until he was within ten feet of where the nine men were settling down to sleep. The talking had ceased.

Raising his head until only his forehead and eyes were above the bank he peered into the darkness at the bandits. It was dark now, the darkness of early night before the moon would rise; there were only the stars to give a faint glow to the landscape. The bandits were all lying down. He studied the shapes and after a while he spotted two, one large and one small, both together and beyond the other shapes. This time his luck was not so good. To reach the girl he would have to crawl past eight bandits. He settled down to wait.

He waited for what he guessed was a full half hour. Already there was a faint glow in the east beyond the hill that was heralding the imminent rise of the moon. He could wait no longer.

There was no sentry. If the nine men were not all sound asleep by now, it couldn't be helped. He raised up and began his crawl, over the bank and toward the first of the sleeping forms. Every foot or so he stopped and listened; he could hear them breathing—one man was snoring like a carpenter wasp eating into a fat pine knot. An inch at a time he slithered past the first dark forms and continued on toward the small form that he hoped was the girl. When one man snorted and rolled over, he froze and lay on his side, so that if seen he would appear to be one of the bandits. After a minute or two he continued on, and some ten minutes later he was within a foot of the small form—it was the little girl.

Inching closer still, so close that he could smell the warm scent of her breath, he placed his lips an inch from her left ear and began to whisper. "Your daddy sent me. Your daddy sent me to get you. Your daddy sent me to get you. Be quiet. Your daddy sent me to get you." He breathed the words, repeating them over and over until at last the little girl stirred and he saw her eyelids flutter and open. "Be quiet. Your daddy sent me to get you. Don't answer. If you understand, follow me and don't make any noise. Touch me with your hand if you understand."

The little girl turned her head and whispered, "I'm tied. My feet are tied to a bush."

Snipe knew she was tied; but he needed her willing cooperation. He whispered back at her, "Stay," and he moved slowly toward her feet, drawing his knife. Carefully he slipped the blade between her ankles and brought it up to the rope and began sawing. The knife was sharp. The rope parted. He sheathed the knife and moved back up to the girl's head and whispered again, "Follow me. Crawl."

He inched his body around and headed back the way he had come. When he had gone three or four feet, he looked back and saw that she was following, crawling on her belly. Children's games. Children were better at this sort of thing than grownups. His confidence rose. And so to a melody played by the creatures of the desert they eased across twenty feet of sand to the wash, down, then east for another twenty feet, where he got to his feet and turned to help the little girl up. "Come," he whispered, and went silently up the wash.

When he reached Kestrel, Snipe turned to the little girl and whispered, "Where are your shoes?"

"He took them so I wouldn't run away."

"Do you know where they are?"

"Yes. He put them in his saddlebag. I don't know where he keeps the saddlebag."

"I'm going back for a rifle," he said to Kestrel. "They're all asleep. It was easy."

"Easy for you," Kestrel said. "Be careful."

Snipe had gone only a few steps when a roar shattered the night. "Up! Up! The girl's gone!" And Snipe whirled around, scooped up the little girl while in full stride, and went running up the wash with Kestrel hard on his heels.

A terrible racket erupted behind them. Guns were fired. A lot of yelling and more guns were fired. Then a loud voice saying, "Go find her! Go!"

By then the two men with the little girl were over a hundred yards away and headed north to circle the hill. The little girl was small and skinny but she was hard-fleshed and to Snipe, who weighed only a hundred and ten pounds himself, the seventy-odd pounds was a heavy load. Another hundred yards and he stopped to tell the girl to get on his back. She did so, and the load was easier to tote. Twenty minutes later they were around the hill, found the burros, set the girl on top of one burro's pack, and off they went toward the east and the rising moon.

CHAPTER NINE

When ex-sergeant Hobart saw that Blount was rattled, he took charge and called the men in. None had gone more than ten feet away from the camp for fear of the unknown. From a sense of security they had gone to one of frozen panic in the toot of a bugle when Blount raised all fallen sinners with his yelling and gun-shooting. Now, five minutes later, they were standing around in the dark, rolling and lighting up smokes and gabbling among themselves like disturbed recruits.

"Who the devil was it?" the cowhand called Jerome said.

Kelly, the other cowhand, who was sometimes a wit, said, "Nobody but some old pullet thief." Nobody laughed.

Hobart slapped his hands together and said in his best drill sergeant's voice, "All right, men. Let's get organized around here. Joe Brown, you and Jerome and Kelly go fetch in the horses. Move it out now. There's nothing or nobody out there to hurt you. Whoever it was is gone. If he'd wanted to cut your throat, he'd've done it ten minutes ago. Now git! Magpie, Forty, Moss, take your guns and go out about fifty feet and stand watch just in case I'm wrong. Stump, build up the fire so we can see what we're doing and put the coffeepot on to settle our nerves. And Blount, let's take a look at where the girl was sleeping."

He struck a lucifer to show his way. "Cut rope. Here's where whoever it was crawled in. And here's where they both crawled away. Whoever it was didn't force the girl to follow him. Notice the crawl sign." The lucifer burnt out. "We got us somebody on our tail, Blount. Who do you think it might be?"

"How the hell would I know, Hobart. You're the sign reader. You tell me." From the sound of his voice it was obvious to Hobart that Blount lacked grit when the going got rough. "You think it wise to light a fire, Hobart?" He added, trying to untangle his tongue.

"They're gone, Blount. Like I told the men, if they'd wanted to cut our throats, they could've done it ten minutes ago. As for me being a sign reader, I'm not. Anybody can read simple sign like this crawl. As for who it was, that's anybody's guess. My guess is it was somebody from Prospect. Nobody else knows we're even out here. And whoever it was knew his job. I could've used a dozen like him back in sixty-four. Could use a few right now too."

"It couldn't have been George Wakefield, could it?" Blount asked, making no endeavor to take back his authority.

"Not likely, Blount. Maybe Injuns. Bounty hunter maybe. He's got the girl, and maybe that's all he was sent for. Then again he might be after the money. I got a hunch we'd better shag ass down the road like we was turpentined mutts.

"No," Blount said. "I want the girl back."

Hobart took a position. "Blount, you're not getting that girl back. Nobody's going after her. We're going to water the horses and load the grub on the mule and hightail it out of here. Is that clear?"

Blount huffed himself up and said, "I reckon that's best, Hobart. You handle things."

"I fully intend to, Blount. Now go get your horse."

Blount made a few false starts and then went out to get his horse.

When he was gone, Hobart said to Stump Brown, "Can you read sign, old-timer?"

"No, but Forty Acre Smith can."

"Hey, Forty! Come on in here." When the old man came in, Hobart asked him if he could read sign.

"I ain't no bygod Injun, sergeant, but I make out."

"Well, light up a torch and see what you can make out. We might find out what we're up against."

The old man took a length of dead ocotillo, lit one end in the fire, and looked around. There had been so many boots going over the sandy ground he found it difficult to pick up anything of note until he followed the crawl marks to the dry wash. There he found moccasin prints and the small prints of the girl's bare feet. "Looks like it was a Injun, sarge. Let's see what's up the wash." He followed the prints up the wash and stopped where another pair of moccasin prints joined the first pair. "Two Injuns. And they're long gone. Take a troop of cavalry to root 'em out and I got my doubts about that."

Hobart couldn't buy Indians. He went back to the

campfire, where the men were standing around holding their horses. He studied their faces in the yellow glow of firelight. They were waiting for him to make the decisions. Even Blount. The full moon had poked its head over the black hill and the landscape was bathed in its soft glow.

"What do you think, sergeant?" Blount asked.

"Well. Forty says there was two of them, both wearing Indian moccasins. There's no doubt they were sent to get the girl, special like. And losing the girl leaves us naked as a peeled skunk. They'll be after the money next. That means we've got to travel. We've got our asses in a tight crack, and a run for Yucca Flat is our only chance. Unless you want to make a stand and fight it out. We could do that if whoever's out there will do everything to suit us and not them. We'll probably run into an ambush sometime before sunup, but that we can't do a thing about. Just keep your guns loaded and handy."

He turned around to look at the four water kegs. Two were empty. One was half full. One was full. "Moss, you and Forty ration out the water in the kegs. One basinful for each horse and what's left goes into the canteens. The rest of you saddle up. We'll pull out in twenty minutes. With any luck at all we ought to get to the next water kegs before sunup."

"Them horses are still bone tired, sergeant," Moss said. He and the cowhands knew horses. "And it's a good twenty miles to the next kegs."

"That's something we can't change, Moss. If you've got nine fresh horses in your pockets, then dig them out. Now let's get at it."

Twenty minutes later they were on their way. Joe

Brown led the way on foot, following the tracks they'd left on the trip north. Hobart took the drag at the tail end, leading the pack mule. He put their chances of getting out of the desert alive at one in about fifty. He'd been in some tight spots before, but he couldn't recall one quite so tight as this one.

CHAPTER TEN

After setting the little girl on one of the burros, Snipe headed east, away from the bandits, and he kept going for over a mile before coming to a halt.

"Hush and listen."

They stood silently for a good five minutes and heard nothing but the normal sounds of the desert night. There were more coyotes in this area than Snipe could remember hearing at one time during all of the past six years in the desert. He and Kestrel had been through this area once before, he remembered now. There was a spring or perhaps even several springs in the area, he reasoned. Given time he could find them all.

"I think we're safe now," he said in his normal speaking voice and looked at the girl. He couldn't see her eyes to read what was behind them. "Are you all right now, miss?" he asked.

"I'm fine, thank you. Will I see my daddy soon?"

Her voice told him more than her words. She would do.

"Not for a little while, miss. Your daddy is still back in Prospect. He didn't come along because he didn't want to hamper us in our search and rescue of you. My name is

Snipe, and my partner's name is Kestrel. We're a couple of birds of a feather." He remembered the girl's name from hearing the marshal say it on the front porch of the banker's house. "Your name is Libby, isn't it? Your daddy told me but I plumb forgot for a moment." He wanted her to talk some more.

"Yes. My name is Libby Wakefield. You're awful brave, aren't you?"

"Not brave, miss. Just sneaky. That's why your daddy sent us to get you, because we have a reputation for being sneaky. We're like the desert fox." He turned to Kestrel. "Can you find your way to Bull Quartz Spring from here, Kes?"

Kestrel knew at once what Snipe had in mind. It was the practical thing to do. He didn't like the idea of Snipe tackling nine heavily armed men alone, yet at the same time he knew that he himself would be of little use at the chore. "I believe I can," he replied and left it at that.

Snipe spoke to the girl. "Miss Libby, Kestrel is going to take you to a pretty place where there's water and shade. You'll see lots of birds and many kinds of desert animals. He'll make you a pair of Indian moccasins and he'll show you lots of little tricks we use to live out here. You'll stay there for about four days, then we'll take you home to your daddy. How does that sound?"

"Are you going to capture those stinky old badmen?"

"I'm going to try my best."

"Don't hurt the boy called Joe, please. He was good to me."

"I'll try not to, miss." He turned to Kestrel. "Give me a hand. I want one of the canvas packs, six full gourds, two spears, the bow and quiver, and don't let me forget the pencil and tablet."

Ten minutes later Snipe was ready. Kestrel added one of the two water reeds, a flint and steel, and a gourd full of saguaro syrup. There was some antelope jerky left, about half a pound, so he added that too. The canvas bags had been originally designed to serve both as backpacks and burro packs. Kestrel didn't ask about what Snipe planned to do because he could pretty well figure it out himself. He did have a suggestion though.

"When you dig up their water kegs, Snipe, don't destroy them. Just roll them a few yards away and rebury them. That way you'll have a water cache in case you need water and can't get it any other way."

"Good idea." Snipe didn't mention that he'd already thought of that. In fact it was an important part of his plan.

They didn't shake hands. Kestrel merely said, "So long, partner," and Snipe said, "I'll see you in about four days. No more than ten at the most." And, taking his direction by the moon, he faced south and took off at a fast lope.

Kestrel waited until he could no longer see Snipe before turning to the girl. "Honey, them nasty old badmen are trying their best right now to catch us, but they won't because we're going to trick them. Now you hang on and don't fall off because we'll be going pretty fast. Here's a water gourd for you. Drink all you want because we've got plenty. Ready?"

"I'm ready, thank you." For Libby Wakefield this was probably the greatest adventure she'd ever have.

"If you want me to stop for any reason just cry out."

"I will, thank you."

Kestrel took the lead burro's leash and faced the North Star. Bull Quartz Spring lay to the southwest a distance of thirty miles. To fool the bandits, or at least give them something to chew on, he intended to go north two or three miles, turn west, then north again, then go around in a circle before crossing the trail of the bandits. Five or six miles farther west he would again turn north and circle back around and set a course to the southwest. It might all be for nought, but he had a child's safekeeping to consider and he was a responsible man.

Meanwhile, to the south, Snipe had already gone a good mile. He knew that he could travel faster on foot than a bunch of tired horses. Still, he also knew that the bandits were disturbed now and would probably think the same thing he was thinking, that whoever got to the next buried water kegs first would win the battle. No, not the battle, merely a skirmish. Now that the little girl was safe, he held so much more of the advantage it was almost unfair. There were ten or more possible skirmishes ahead and he need only win one of them; the bandits had to win them all.

He was feeling physically fit and was running easy. The moonlight allowed him to see ahead clearly for a distance of fifty feet, and not so clearly he could make out brooding hills long before he got to them. Desert creatures got out of his way like twin waves from the bow of a fast-speeding boat. All but the rattlesnakes. And because of the possibility of rattlesnakes he kept watching the ground ahead and avoided anything that resembled one of the critters. One misstep could lose him the whole battle.

This desolate land with its almost evenly spaced shrubs and plants seemed especially designed for a running man. There was little wonder that the Apaches had developed into such excellent foot travelers. The ground was almost uniformly level, with few things to trip a running man. He was no longer amazed at the fighting tenacity of the Apaches who owned this land in friendly enmity with the passive, more gentle Papagos. Were it his land, he would fight just as hard to keep it.

As he loped through a vast field of bur sage, skirting clumps of organpipe cactus, he asked himself if his desire to own land below the border was truly sincere. Was it not more that all men must have a goal somewhere in the future that was barely obtainable? Even the richest of men were unsatisfied with what they possessed. It seemed that there had to be something out there just beyond reach, beckoning, always just beyond the reaching fingertips. He tried to visualize a small black man dickering for a piece of land with people whose language he did not understand. Would they truly accept him? And if so, how many years would it take to meld himself into their society so that he and they were the same. Five years? Ten? There would be hurdles ahead. Obstructions that even gold could not breach. There would never be quite enough money. The man with ten thousand dollars always could find need for ten thousand more.

Would he not be better off to contract for one of the girls of the Papagos, a girl accustomed to the desert life? They were a gentle people, the Papagos. Their customs seemed especially designed for the hard and sometimes harsh life of desert dwellers. The Papago will share his last tepary bean with a friend. He will never lie to you, for a lie might prove disastrous. He would of course be required by a Papago wife to live among the people, for only a closely knit group could survive. He would need to learn all of the customs and ways of his wife's people, in essence become a Papago himself.

What was it exactly that made the Papagos such a gentle people? Was it that they held no wants beyond the simple needs of everyday living? He could think of no other reason. Cast aside all craving for riches, all you greedy people of the world, and live the simple life that nature intended. He smiled at the thought.

Bearing gradually toward the right and on the watch for the tracks, he went on and came upon them after a distance of perhaps eight miles—it had not cost him the time it would have cost had he turned right in the beginning. He stopped, drank from one of the six gourds, took a generous swallow of syrup, and continued at a slower pace. The slower pace was his way of resting between runs. He was ahead of the bandits, but he had no idea how far ahead. He would need at least an hour to dig up the water kegs when he found the campsite.

His thoughts returned to the future. The more he thought about life as a Papago Indian maiden's husband, the more it appealed to him. There would be no need to embrace their social customs exclusively. Perhaps he could safely add a few customs of his own and those of his father the African Bushman. He felt that he had something to contribute. The Papagos were seminomads, moving from place to place as the demands of game foods dictated.

His thoughts shifted when he spotted something white high up on one trunk of a cluster of organpipe cactus ahead. It was the campsite. Soon he was on ground trampled by many boots and horseshoes. The full moon lay far over to the west. He estimated that dawn was at most an hour away. Yes, the big dipper was way over, pouring water down its handle, and the morning star had risen.

Even in the bright moonlight he was unable after ten minutes or so to find the spot where the kegs were buried. The ground was a mixture of broken desert rocks and sand. He searched frantically for the water keg grave and could not find it. He would have to probe. At the previous campsite the tops of the kegs had been only a few inches below the ground level. Maybe his knife with its six-inch blade would do. He began at the most likely burial site near the organpipe and began probing.

It was full daylight when at last the knife point struck wood. He sheathed the knife and began digging with his hands. The once loosened desert earth came out easily, and within minutes he had one keg lifted out of its hole.

He felt that he was sorely pressed for time. The distance from the previous campsite was shorter than he had expected, at most fifteen miles. Even tired horses could go that distance in the cool of one night.

With the one keg out of its nest, he rolled it some thirty yards away and began at once to dig a new hole for it. It seemed to take forever to get the hole deep enough. With a proper shovel he could have dug a hole deep enough for one ten-gallon keg in five minutes. This one took half an hour. When he had the first keg buried and the loose earth smoothed over the hole, he stood up and looked north. There were too many tall organpipes and mesquites and creosote bushes obstructing his view. The sun was already up. He drank from one of his gourds and decided to chance one more keg.

First he found out how many there were—four. Then he dug a hole for the second keg, after which he uncovered the keg and rolled it to the ready-made hole. He had it buried and had brush-swept the whole area prior to tackling a third keg when he heard a noise not often heard in the desert—the snort of a tired horse.

Without bothering to look, he snatched up his spears and quiver and pack and fled. He ran for two hundred yards toward the sun, hoping it would serve to blind anyone looking his way, before he stopped to hide behind a mesquite tree.

He waited, and listened. He heard another snort, then a voice followed by more voices. He could not make out the words. He left, keeping the mesquite between himself and the campsite. He went a good mile before stopping to look around. There wasn't a hill of any size closer than ten miles. There was one far to the south, which he knew was Black Hill One.

Going back the way he had come for twenty paces, he inspected the hard ground. He had left no prints, none but a few disturbed desert pavement rocks which only an expert tracker would notice. Good enough. He chose a thickly branched paloverde tree and took shelter on the west side to wait and think.

He was disappointed with his performance. He could have traveled faster, got here sooner. His plan was wrecked. One Palm Spring was only about thirty more miles to the south and there might not be another campsite short of there with buried kegs. With two kegs of water the bandits could make it that far. And there they could stay as long as they cared to stay to rest the horses and themselves before going on. Damn!

He rummaged in the pack for the jerky and bit off a chunk. With the bandits in all likelihood searching for him, he didn't dare hunt for meat he would have to cook. Jerky and syrup would have to do.

He needed a new plan. But first, what would the bandits do when they discovered the two missing kegs? Would they extend the search for him? Had they seen him? He doubted that, or they would have chased him on their horses. Would they spend the day sleeping and resting the horses and then go on after dark, which was the smart thing to do? He decided they would. How far was it to the next campsite and buried water kegs, providing there was another campsite between here and One Palm Spring? How far was the next campsite. Ten miles? Twenty? Halfway?

He took count of his resources. Two spears. Bow with twenty-one arrows. Two full water gourds. Four empty. Half a gourd full of syrup. Jerky. Knife. Water reed. The water would barely last out the day.

He told himself to think.

He thought hard for an hour and gave up to get some sleep. At midday he moved to the east side of the tree and sat chewing jerky. His now-aborted plan had been to rebury all of the kegs and leave a message impaled on a spine of the organpipe cactus to the effect that he would give them the location of the kegs in return for their guns and the money. That would have been tricky to pull off. It was not a good plan at all—he realized that now. He had planned to watch them from a hiding place, and around here there was no hiding place high enough for him to look down on them. No, in this location it wasn't a good plan at all. He no longer felt disappointed that he hadn't been able to bring it off. At least he had deprived them of two kegs.

Now what?

He did some more thinking as the shadow of the paloverde tree grew longer and longer. The shadow reached out for all of twenty feet when a new plan leaped into his head full grown. He jumped to his feet, for he didn't have more time to waste. He drank half the water in the last gourd and gathered up spears and bow and quiver and headed south.

Two miles and he turned west toward the trail. He felt pleased when he saw that all the hoofprints pointed north. The gods were being good to him again. He went south down the trail, searching for an ideal spot for an ambush. He had to go another mile and the sunlight was beginning to fade when he found a spot that would do.

Making note of a large clump of organpipe cactus some twenty feet west of the trail, he went on for another three hundred yards to a spot that would do for the second ambush. After a thorough inspection of the second spot, he went back to the first and settled down on the west side of the organpipe cactus to wait.

While there was still light enough to see by, he selected his four best arrows and laid them on the ground. Then he strung the bow and tested it. What he was about to do didn't please him at all. For one thing it was very chancy.

But most of all he didn't enjoy hurting horses. He searched his brain for an alternative plan. None came.

He waited, and while waiting he chewed jerky and resisted the urge to drink the rest of his water. He sipped saguaro syrup, which only made his thirst more intense. It was still hot an hour after sunset. There was no breeze at all. There had been no mourning doves calling before sunset. Now the only night sound was the yipping of a single coyote. No springs in this area.

He had a long wait. The moon had been up for an hour when he heard hoofbeats. He got ready. His ambush spot was on the west side of the south end of the clump of organpipe. From here he could shoot at an angle that would hide him from the bandits on horseback unless they chanced to look back. He nocked an arrow and gripped three more with his left hand. The two spears were on the ground, ready in case he needed them.

The horses were close. He saw a man on foot at the point position, followed by the man's horse and then the first man on horseback. He began to count them. One on foot. Two. Three. Four. Five. Six. Seven. Get ready. He drew back the bowstring. Eight. Nine. He let fly at the third to last horse and had a second arrow nocked when the horse screamed. Thawk!—the second arrow hit the eighth horse. Thawk! Down went the last horse in line as he snatched up his spears and fled, keeping the organpipe between himself and the bandits.

He was a hundred feet from the ambush when the shooting started. He heard the distinctive vacuum swack as bullets went past his head. He zigzagged and kept running until the shooting stopped.

Circling to the west and then south and then east, he

arrived at the second ambush spot while the bandits were still rattled and milling around in disorder up the trail.

He took a position on the east of the trail, behind a single barrel cactus that stood about four feet high. He had chosen this almost open spot because he knew the bandits would be inspecting all truly likely ambush spots after losing three horses.

For the second ambush he would fire only one arrow. That was all the time he dared to take. The bandits would surely be alert and quick to shoot at shadows. One shot and scoot.

He had a long wait. It was a full hour before he heard hoofbeats coming. He hunkered down with an arrow nocked. Three men on foot went by. They all had rifles ready to shoot. He let them go and counted three men with the horses. Then the mule. Then the last three men went by, also armed with rifles. He let the last three men get a good twenty yards down the trail and then shot at the mule.

While the arrow was still in flight, he snatched up the spears and scampered away. The mule didn't scream the way the horses had done. All it did was grunt. But the instant it grunted, the bullets starting flying. He got up on his toes and fairly flew past the desert plants into the night. With every step he knew that the next bullet would get him in the back. He heard yells and the pounding of boots. When the firing stopped, he headed back toward the campsite to fill his water gourds.

CHAPTER ELEVEN

Hobart knew when they found that two of their water kegs had been swiped that they were in worse trouble than anyone had imagined. The man or men dogging their rumps across the desert were elusive as coyotes, tricky as wolverines, and fast on their feet or their horses. He still couldn't figure out even what it was doing all the mischief.

The cool night trip from the last campsite had been slow but downright pleasant. Even the horses had perked up. Before reaching this campsite shortly after sunup, he had expressed hope that the girl was all the tricky coyotes had been after. Now he knew better. They were up against somebody who used the desert the way a gambler uses a deck of marked cards.

"It was the same men," Forty Acre Smith said after examining the moccasin prints around the hole where the two remaining water kegs had been buried. "One of them anyhow. Same patch on the sole of his left foot."

Blount, who hadn't been saying much, piped up with, "If there's only two of them, let's set a trap and pick them off why don't we?"

Hobart looked at the big man with contempt. "You know something, Blount? Just because you're stupid, you think everybody else is stupid too. How can we set a trap when we can do nothing but play the game their way? Answer me that, you hog."

"You ain't got no cause to pick on me, Hobart. You're in this deep as I am."

"To my everlasting shame," and Hobart turned away to look over the horses with Moss.

The tough little mustangs were in bad shape. All were sorefooted. They all had a last-legs hangdog look about them.

"We mistreated them poor beasts," Moss said as they watched the horses trying to feed on dry desert grass and mesquite beans. "They could use twice, hell, four times the water they been getting. We sure got roped into a cold-deck game if you was to ask me."

"Don't go piling all the blame on Blount," Hobart said. "We roped ourselves in. Now how are we gonna get out? That's the last-card question."

"What galls me is we can't get a look at the hole cards of the whatever it is out there pestering us," Moss moaned. "We ain't seen a hair of them yet. Like bloody ghosts they are. You reckon there is ghosts out here?"

Hobart turned his back on the horses and gazed at the men sprawled around the campfire waiting for grub. "They're real enough, Moss. What I can't figure is why they don't pick us off."

"Could be they ain't got no guns," Moss speculated.

"Naw," Hobart said with exasperation and a shake of his head. Then he gave it some thought. "Yeah. That might be it. For all the good it does us. Can't figure any other reason. I bet there's a price on our heads by now. Outlaws. Makes a body sit up and think a bit, don't it?"

"How'll the law know who we are?"

"They don't have to know what our names are, old hoss. That wart on a donkey's ass over there didn't say a word about him knowing that banker before we hit that bank. Now we're part of the Gower Blount outlaw gang. Bank robbers. Little-girl takers. Folks don't take kindly to men like us." He shook his head. "I oughta be locked up in the crazy house."

Moss kicked the ground with a boot toe and said, "Hobart, what say you and me take off and head west or east or something. This here trail we're on is spooked."

"I've been mulling about just that, old buddy. Blount was telling me about a spring over to the west a piece that yahoo working the arrastra told him about. Ten miles west of Black Hill Two, he said it was. And that's Black Hill One right down yonder. Makes it about thirty miles all told. We could lay up there and wait for the heat to cool off."

"When we going?" Moss asked.

"How about tonight?"

"What's wrong with right now?"

"Moss, you ain't got the brain God gave a worm. Without water them horses won't go a mile. Come night we'll tag along like we was going all the way, then we sort of branch off this side of that black hill."

"I wasn't paying no heed to them horses."

"That's your trouble, Moss. You don't pay no heed." Hobart kept looking at Blount. "I sure do hate to let that tub of lard get away with half the take though. He never earned no half share. How much did he put up for the horses and grub and guns? A thousand at the most. I figure he owes us maybe another thousand apiece."

"Go ask him for it, Hobart. I'll back you up."

"I think I bygod will at that." Hobart went over to stand in front of Blount, who was lying in the shade with his head on his saddle. "Blount, me and Moss figure you owe us another thousand apiece. Get it up."

Blount didn't move. He lay there with one of his black dog's hind leg cigars in his jaw and looked up at Hobart. The other men lying around didn't say a word.

"I said get it up, Blount."

Blount rolled his head from side to side to look at the other men. Eight thousand dollars growing wings and learning how to fly. Eight from twelve leaves four. He was about to get rooked in his own game. A busted flush on the last card.

"Help yourself," he said. "In my saddlebags."

"What about us?" Kelly the cowhand said.

"Help yourself," Blount repeated.

Hobart grinned at Moss and reached down for the saddlebags. "I'll just count it out in eight neat little piles, boys. Anybody want to keep tally?"

"Naw. We trust you, sergeant. Don't we, boys?"

"Yeah."

Blount said, "Take it all. We ain't none of us going to live to spend it."

"How so?" Hobart asked.

"The men who dug up the kegs know we buried kegs at every camp. They're going ahead of us. Plain enough for any fool to see. And without water we're all dead."

"That's right, men," Forty Acre Smith said. "We done bought us a mail-order headstone. Had that figured soon as I spotted that half-empty hole when we rode up. What I can't figure is how did they know the kegs was buried."

"I've been puzzling that out for the past hour," Blount said, raising himself up to a sitting position. "And I think I got the answer. Can't be anything else. The only men who saw them kegs on the mules besides us was them two at that place with the one palm tree and the spring."

"That little runt?"

"Yep. That little runt."

"Now I ain't about to buy that, Blount," Hobart said. "Where did you get the kegs in the first place?"

"I bought the kegs over six months ago down in Arizona Territory and hauled them up to where they were stashed and we picked them up. Nobody but me knew about the kegs. Nobody."

Hobart had to believe it. He'd seen the condition of the kegs there in the cave, covered with dust and filled with water to keep them from dry warping. After they loaded them on the mules, nobody saw them but the little runt and his partner they'd seen at the spring. Blount had no reason to lie about it.

Hobart looked at the faces around him. "Anybody see anybody else on the trip?"

The men all shook their heads no.

"Anybody tell anybody in Prospect? No, I know the answer to that. Forty, how far is it to that spring from here?"

"Thirty miles, give or take."

"When we get there I'm gonna peel me a bygod runt." Hobart turned to Moss. "What can we do for the horses?"

"Love 'em up a lot and treat 'em like royalty is about all. Then go easy and slow. And give them more water. Won't hurt us none to rustle up some feed for them too."

"All right. On your feet, men. You too, Blount. Get out there and fetch them horses under the shade and then go round up everything that looks fit for a horse to eat. Now move it."

As the sun arched across the sky, they coddled the nine horses and one pack mule. Hobart drove them out into the skillet-hot sun and lashed them with his tongue when they slowed down. The men gathered bur sage and mesquite beans and prickly-pear pads and fetched them to the horses.

Kelly and Joe Brown got fed up with bean picking and decided as a joke to fetch in a whole barrel cactus six feet long and a foot thick. They first trimmed off the spines, chopped it off near the ground, and hefted it the way they would a log. It seemed to weigh a ton. When they got it to the horses and chopped off chunks, they were surprised as was Hobart when the horses took to it like hogs to sweet potatoes. The barrel cactus pulp was heavy with moisture, the sap that was very much like water fairly dripping out of it.

"Hey! They like it!"

"Look at 'em gobble it down!"

They had made a lifesaving discovery. The horses perked up. And by the time the sun was setting and the men were exhausted, the horses were even a bit frisky.

When Blount proposed that they start before sundown Hobart said, "No, no hurry. No rush. Wait for the moon. Long time to next daylight. We'll take her slow and easy."

His authority drew the men together in a way they had never been before. It seemed as though he was using baling wire to hold them together. He estimated that their chances had improved and were now one in five of getting out of the desert alive. He'd gone against those kind of odds a lot of times.

When the moon was an hour high and they were able to see a hundred feet or more, he said, "All right, men. We'll ride a mile and walk a mile. Give the horses a break. Joe Brown, you take the lead on foot. And don't walk too fast, you hear."

Necessity was forcing them to learn how to live in the desert. It was something they couldn't fight and expect to win. The heat and dryness were relentless, but the elements wouldn't kill unless the men helped get the job done. The barrel cactus had saved the horses, and in so doing had saved the men.

Joe Brown led off on foot, leading his horse, and the others fell in behind him. Already the air was getting cool. They set a slow pace, a steady plodding that would take them ten to fifteen miles before next daylight.

Hobart, bringing up the rear, was feeling self-satisfied with what he had accomplished. He was looking forward to the next buried water kegs, praying that they would still be there. One more camp and then the spring. If the pesky runt wasn't there, he'd wait for him if it took a year. He'd peel the hide off the little bastard, whack his bygod gonads off. Learn him not to fiddle around with Sergeant Jason Hobart.

Some three miles south of the camp, where the moon was casting long shadows across the trail, the horse two places forward of Hobart suddenly squealed like a scalded pig and leaped into the air to come down bucking and snorting. What the hell? About then the horse directly ahead toppled over, squealing and kicking.

Hobart whirled around to draw his rifle from its scabbard and jacked a shell into firing position. As he was looking around for something to shoot at, his own horse rared up and fell over backwards, making a gawdawful racket. Still he couldn't see anything to shoot at. He had no idea what was happening. Then he caught a glimpse of a running shadow back and to the west and sent a bullet at it. He ran after the shadow, firing his rifle as fast as he could pump shells. Moss joined him and cut loose. They ran a hundred feet and kept firing until their guns were empty.

"Hold it, Moss! Back to the horses."

They rushed back and found three horses down, still kicking and squealing.

"What the devil ails the blasted critters?" Hobart asked of Forty Acre Smith.

Magpie found an arrow lodged up to its feathers in the guts of his horse. "Gutshot, sergeant," he said. "Done for. Might as well shoot 'em."

"Save your lead," Hobart told him, remembering the time back in Tennessee when his whole platoon ran out of shot for their palmetto muskets. He handed his rifle to Moss and, drawing his knife, he slit his own horse's throat. When he raised up, he said to Magpie and Forty, "Well, get at it."

It took Hobart an hour getting the men organized again. Saddlebags were lifted off the three dead horses and put on the pack mule. "Take what you can tote," he told them. "But don't leave behind any ammunition. If we run into more trouble up ahead, you'll wish you'd left the bygod gold behind instead." He was thinking that there wasn't a way on God's earth they could avoid trouble up ahead. Still, he was feeling an elation he hadn't felt since his last battle of the war. He was more alive than he'd been in sixteen years. It was almost a pleasure to slit the throats of the horses and order the men to load the saddlebags on the mule. Six horses and the mule left. Nobody hurt.

When they were ready to renew the march, Hobart put three men on point and kept three men for drag. "Be ready to shoot fast," he told them. "The sneaky bastard's trying to put us all on foot. Look sharp! Move it out. Hoooooo!" He sounded almost cheerful.

They started off, every man on foot, the horses and pack mule strung out like linked sausages between two groups of men at the head and tail with ready rifles. Nothing happened for three hundred yards or so. Then the mule gave a grunt. And the instant he heard the grunt, Hobart whirled around and spotted a dodging shadow back and to the east. He fired one quick shot and took off in pursuit. Magpie and Moss went with him, spraying bullets ahead of them. They ran as fast as they could in their high-heeled riding boots but it wasn't fast enough. A hundred yards and Hobart called a halt. They went back and found the others gathered around the downed pack mule.

Cursing an enemy he couldn't draw a bead on, Hobart slit the mule's throat and had the men load the grub and gear on the six horses. When everything was ready once again, he said, "Move it out," and they went on down the trail to what they all thought would be endless ambushes.

No more ambushes occurred, that night.

CHAPTER TWELVE

When Snipe got back to the bandits' campsite, he dug up one of the two water kegs he'd buried and filled his six water gourds. He drank all he could hold before reburying the keg. Water wasn't enough; his body was telling him that he needed food. He hadn't eaten a filling meal since sharing the tortoise with Kestrel. So he hurried south down the trail to where three horses lay dead.

A pack of coyotes were already gnawing at the bellies. He chased the coyotes away and set to work on one horse with his knife. Slicing down the brisket and up the shank, he peeled back the hide and cut out about six pounds of flank steaks. These he cut into foot-long strips and took them about two hundred yards west of the trail and built a fire of dead cactus wood behind a clump of organpipe cactus. He built up the fire to a roaring blaze, let it die down to glowing coals, and laid on the horse steaks. They sizzled and flared up and charred quickly. When they were well blackened, he lifted them off, put all but one strip into his backpack, tucked the two spears under one arm with the points forward so the other ends would drag on the ground, and went back to the trail and turned south.

He ate flank steak as he went along at a fast walk. The horsemeat had a strong flavor that was only partially suppressed by the charring. He'd eaten a lot worse meat. It wasn't exactly top eating, but it was filling and within a mile he could feel the new energy and strength flowing through his body.

When he'd eaten all he could hold, he topped the meat off with a swallow of saguaro syrup and drank some water. He kept on at a fast walk until the meat gave him enough strength to get up on his toes once again to pick up the loping gait that fitted him so well.

The area of relatively dense desert plants and trees that was caused by a shallow water table soon gave way to flatland speckled with bur sage and the ubiquitous creosote bush. Here he could see the tracks clearly and see ahead nearly a hundred yards in the washing moonlight. He reckoned the time by the position of the big dipper at close to midnight. He would have to go faster if he was to get around the bandits and beat them to the next buried water kegs or One Palm Spring, whichever came first. He put on more speed and lengthened his stride. A spear in each hand gave him better balance and forward thrust—it was very much as if he was reaching forward and pulling himself along by the weight of the spears.

About three miles south of the dead horses he spotted the bandits up ahead. Killing the horses and the mule had done what he had hoped it would do, slow them down. He slowed to a walk and left the trail to circle around to the west. The going was just as easy, and ten minutes later he was ahead of the bandits and once again he picked up the pace.

As he loped along he thought about Kestrel and the little girl. At this moment they were probably some ten miles northeast of Bull Quartz Spring. Kestrel would travel slow, making no more than ten to fifteen miles between sundown and sunup. During the first daylight camp he had probably made the girl a pair of moccasins so that she could walk beside him. Kestrel was the sort to be good with kids. He had the patience and a lot of the ways of a mother. Sometimes he could be downright exasperating the way he fussed. A good partner, though. He cared. Snipe had got snakebit once and Kestrel had done for him better than most doctors and had nursed him afterwards as good as any woman. He was a good cook too, when they were not on the go. Once in a while he would bake a cake, using corn flour and saguaro syrup. Smacking good eating.

Snipe became suddenly conscious that he was slowing down again. He tried to increase the pace and found he could not. He needed food again. He got out the syrup gourd, took a healthy swig, and dug out another flank steak. Charred hours ago, it wasn't very tasty, hardly fit to eat, but he forced it down anyway. He was determined to get to the next campsite in plenty of time to dig up the water kegs, rebury them, and write a message for the bandits to chew on when they showed up. All depending on there being another campsite short of the spring.

It was about two hours later when he spotted the shape of a three-armed saguaro up ahead in the slanting moonlight and a moment later he saw the white rag. More good luck. He knew that he was no more than eight or ten miles north of One Palm Spring.

The time of night was about an hour before first daylight. The moon was three fingers high in the west, casting a good light on the ground around the saguaro. Quickly he put down the spears and pack and began probing with his knife. The point struck wood on the fifth probe. The ground was almost pure sand. Digging was easy. In half an hour he had four kegs dug up. He filled the hole and then rolled the kegs in four different directions a distance of forty to sixty yards.

Prying the bung out of one keg, he filled his water gourds and set to work to bury the kegs. It took him until good daylight to get them all underground. He then cut a brush broom from an ironwood tree and swept the whole area.

Satisfied that the bandits would have a difficult time finding the kegs, he dug out the pencil stub and writing tablet and sat down to compose a message.

I WILL TRADE 4 KEGS OF WATER FOR YOUR GUNS AND THE MONEY. IF ALL NINE OF YOU AGREE, TAKE DOWN THE WHITE RAG. I WILL COME TO YOU AND WE WILL TALK. IF YOU SHOOT ME YOU WILL ALL DIE OF THIRST.

He signed it with a pictograph of a snipe bird and read it over twice. It would be easy for them to trick him, but that was a chance he'd have to take. If they were thirsty enough, and they would be, the chances of them shooting him he estimated at about one in a hundred.

Taking one of his arrows from the quiver, he impaled the message on the saguaro above the spot where he'd dug up the kegs and then left, headed toward the rising sun. The desert floor here was too sandy even to try hiding his footprints. He continued east until he came to harder ground, where he turned south and circled around the campsite. Off to the west stood Black Hill Two, about one mile west of the campsite. From its eastern slope he would be able to look down on the bandits.

As he headed for Black Hill Two, he thought about the message and the bandits. They would not give up the money easily. No man does that. He had little hope that they would. Still, he had to offer them the chance to save themselves. Eight of the nine men could well be basically honest men who had fallen victim to an offer of easy money. He and Kestrel could well have been two of them under the same circumstances. He had given much thought to the few minutes in the bank with the bandits and had reached the probability that the man called Blount was mad, the way that all seekers of vengeance are mad. Had he not rescued the little girl, Blount would very likely have killed her out of spite and revenge.

The sun was well up when he reached the foot of Black Hill Two. Like most desert hills in this area, it was bare black volcanic rock except for the lower slopes, which were sprinkled with giant saguaros mixed with ironwood trees and the ever-present creosote bush. Here and there were patches of brittlebush. He went up the slope and stopped above the last vegetation and turned to look back. The whole desert floor lay open below, stretching on and on as if there was no end to it. He settled in the shade of a saguaro to watch the white rag.

CHAPTER THIRTEEN

"What kind of bird is that, Mr. Kestrel?" the little girl asked.

"Where?"

"Up on that big tree."

"The big tree is a saguaro cactus, honey, and the bird is a Gila woodpecker. Gilas and flickers make their nests inside the saguaro. See all the holes up there. The woodpeckers make the holes and, when they move out, other birds move in."

Kestrel was finding the little girl a delight, chiefly because she made him feel more knowledgeable than he thought he really was. She was full of curiosity and questions about every bush, every tree, every cactus plant, every animal and snake and bird.

"What kind of other birds?"

"Oh, elf owls, flycatchers. Let me see. Purple martins. Even bats. See that big nest way over there on top of that saguaro? That's a hawk's nest. Redtail hawk. There he is now. Pretty bird, the hawk. There's a hawk called the kestrel. Me and Snipe were born in the same year and we were named after birds by our folks."

"Will we stop soon?"

"In a little bit. I'm looking for a good-size tree so we'll be in the shade."

"A paloverde tree like yesterday morning?"

"Yes. Or a big mesquite or ironwood or even a big clump of organpipe cactus. That ironwood up there looks promising."

The sun had been up for only a few minutes and already the dew was gone from the bushes they passed. The land was flat for as far as they could see in all directions, with not a hill anywhere to be seen. They had been in a saguaro forest for the past three hours and it appeared as if they would still be in it for hours after night came again. Among the stately saguaros around them were cholla cactus, mesquite, paloverde, ironwood, barrel cactus, and creosote bush.

The first night, after Snipe had left them, they had traveled fast and had covered at least twenty-five miles, which had actually been about ten miles as the crow flies. After resting during the heat of the day, they had come on and had covered another ten miles or so. By all accounts Bull Quartz Spring should be no more than ten miles ahead. It should be, but he wasn't so sure that it was. He had never been in this area before. Always he and Snipe had come upon Bull Quartz Spring from the south or west or southwest, never from the northeast. His sense of direction was not nearly so good as Snipe's. Not that he was worried. There was a good way to find the spring from here. Now and for the past hour, since first daylight, he'd been hearing mourning doves calling. And he'd seen several pairs flying overhead, on their way to water for their morning drink. He need only follow the doves.

Bull Quartz Hill was not a place one could see from a far distance. The pile of white boulders stood only about forty feet high and covered an area of no more than ten acres. That mere dab of hill set in the middle of hundreds of square miles of desert was never easy to find.

"Do you think Mr. Snipe has captured those old badmen yet?"

"He doesn't intend to capture them, honey. They've got lots of guns and Snipe has only his bow and two spears. He's going to try to make them capture themselves."

"How?"

Kestrel went around a big cholla cactus that had a dozen or more cactus wren nests in it and saw ahead the ironwood tree. It was good and bushy and lived alongside a giant saguaro with four arms raised up as if beseeching alms from heaven. He was glad to see the thickly foliaged ironwood, for the morning sun was getting very hot.

"I don't know just how he'll do it, honey, not exactly."

"There's a rattlesnake."

"Where?"

"There."

He looked at where she was pointing. She was riding the second burro. Following the pointing finger, he saw the rattler coiled under a creosote bush. It had two big lumps along its body that indicated it had captured and swallowed two pack rats or small rabbits during the night.

"Breakfast," Kestrel said, dropping the lead rope to slide out the spear from the first burro's pack. He went over to the snake and dragged it out and beat it to death.

He cut off the head and squeezed out the prey—they were baby jackrabbits. He draped the still-squirming snake over the first burro's pack and buried the snake's head before going on to the ironwood tree. Burying the head was from habit; a severed snake's head was still dangerous should someone step on it.

"We're in luck, honey. A spot all cleared out for us."

He took the pack off the first burro, set it on the ground in the shade, then he lifted the girl off and set her on the pack. "I'll make you some moccasins for sure today, honey. I was just too fagged out yesterday morning."

"I was too."

"Do you need to make water?"

"Yes, please."

He picked her up again and carried her around the tree and out about twenty feet. Before standing her down he used one moccasin-clad foot to smooth away any bur sage seeds. "Call me when you've finished." He went back around the ironwood tree.

For the next five minutes or so he gazed up at the air, looking for flying doves. It was about the right time for them to be flying back from their morning drink. He saw one pair way off to the west but he couldn't make out their true flight path. The girl called and he went to get her.

As he sat her down on the pack he said, "Honey, you can help me. While I make camp, you can keep a lookout for doves flying overhead. When you see one, call me quick so I can see it before it gets too far away. For the most part they fly in pairs. Will you do that for me?"

"Why?"

Kestrel took a position. "Because I'm not real positive sure where we are, honey."

"Will the doves tell you where we are?"

"Yes."

"How?"

Kestrel smiled at her. "Well, suppose you keep a lookout for flying doves and I'll tell you how while I get breakfast."

"All right." She raised her eyes.

While he unloaded the second burro and turned them both loose to browse, he told her about doves. "When you're lost in the desert, where there are doves, all you have to do is watch the flying doves in the early morning and again in the late afternoon. Doves need water at least once a day and often twice a day if the weather is hot like it is now. Needing water so often, they nest in places close enough to water to fly there and back in a short time.

"Now doves can fly fairly fast. I suppose one can fly ten miles in ten to twenty minutes. That's guesswork, but ten miles in twenty minutes is probably right. Very well, so you watch the doves. They usually fly a straight course going to water and a straight course flying back to their nesting and feeding grounds.

"Sometimes just one pair of doves is enough to tell you not only in which direction water is, but just how far it is too. For example, you see a pair of doves flying in one direction at first daylight; they are probably the first pair of doves to fly in that direction from where you are that morning. You wait, and keep track of the time, and when a pair of doves comes back from that direction you make note of the time. If the time is say one half hour, you divide that by two to get the flying time for one direction. Allow only about ten seconds for drinking because doves drink very fast. They suck up water the same as a burro does. It took the doves fifteen minutes one way. Taking a dove's speed at thirty miles per hour, you will know that the spring or watering place is about eight miles away."

He grinned. "And I hope that's clear to you, honey, because I'm nothing but confused. I never was very good at fancy arithmetic anyway."

"What if there's more than one pair of doves?"

"You mean flying in different directions?"

"Yes."

"In that case you use your water reed and forget about the doves."

"Water reed? You can get water with a water reed?"

"Yep. That reed right there. Willow stick. Hollow. You find a spot where cottonwood trees are growing and you're cold out guaranteed to get water with a water reed. If there ain't no cottonwoods, you look for a dry wash with bigger than usual trees, say a paloverde that looks like it gets more water than the average paloverde. That means the roots are getting plenty of water. So you dig a hole three or four feet deep in the wash near the paloverde tree, down till you hit moist sand. That's all it has to be, moist, not sopping wet.

"Gather you some dry grass, say a double handful, stuff it down in the bottom of the hole in a tight wad, poke the end of your water reed into the center of the ball of dry grass, then cover the whole thing up with the sand you got out of the hole. Then you just lay down on your belly and suck on the end of the water reed. You know what happens down there where the wad of grass is?"

"No. Tell me."

"When you suck on the reed, it builds up a suction in the wad of grass, the suction pulls the water out of the moist sand into the wad of grass, and you suck the water right up through the reed into your mouth and there you are. Water."

"Golly. You mean we've got to get water like that?"

"We might if we don't see some doves all flying the same direction come early evening."

"Are we really lost right now?"

"Not on your life, honey. I'm just not exactly sure where we are, like I just said." He emptied one of the canvas bags and spread it on the ground in the shade for her to sit on. She looked sleepy. "I'll gather some firewood now before it gets too hot. Drink all the water you want. We've got plenty." He went wood gathering. There was plenty of dead cactus wood, the skeletons of cholla cactus mostly. When he came back with an armload she was asleep. He dumped the wood ten feet away from her because scorpions make their homes in dead cactus wood and one could crawl out and sting her.

Digging out the big copper pot, he put some tepary beans on to soak. Then he skinned the rattler, cut it up, and salted the pieces. He mixed corn flour for flapjacks in the little tea-making pot and only then did he build a fire and put the big iron skillet on. No sense burning firewood needlessly, even when it was plentiful.

He roasted the snake by dropping the pieces directly in the fire and letting them get charred. He cooked two flapjacks for himself and ate them with syrup. He also ate three pieces of snake. He considered letting the girl sleep but decided to wake her up because she needed food. But before he woke her, he fried her two flapjacks, wiped the corn flour out of the little pot, and boiled joint-fir tea. The syrup served very well for long sweetening for the tea. When he had everything ready to eat, he shook her awake.

The girl ate with good appetite, which pleased him. She didn't look like the sickly type of child, more the opposite. She looked healthy as a young filly.

"I'm sorry I fell asleep, Mr. Kestrel."

"That's all right, honey. We'll watch for doves this afternoon late, just before sunset."

"All right." She mopped up her plate, ate two joints of snake, drank a mug of sweetened tea, and fell asleep almost immediately after.

While the girl slept and the tepary beans bubbled away in the big pot, he dug out the moccasin-mending bag and started on her moccasins. He measured her right foot for length and width and cut out ten sole and heel patterns. Each moccasin would have six layers of leather for the sole and heel. For himself and Snipe he used ten layers glued together with piñon pitch.

He was engrossed with sewing the primary sole and heel to the leggins when the two burros came looking for shade. He told them howdy do and the dominant jenny wiggled her ears at him.

It took him all morning to finish the little moccasins. By then the sun was directly overhead. It was very hot and still. All around he could see dust devils dancing their way among the desert plants. The creosote bushes were giving off their faint odor.

Holding up the moccasins, he admired his handicraft. A Papago woman wouldn't have them in her hut. They looked crude. But they were good and stout and would last the girl a long time.

"Hey! Honey! Wake up!" He shook her by her arm. When she opened her eyes he said, "Time to shift around to the other side of the tree. Look what I made for you." He gave her the moccasins. "Put them on and you can walk around to the other side like a big girl. No more being carried everywhere. Like 'em?"

"They're real nice. Thank you, Mr. Kestrel."

"Go ahead. Put 'em on. That one's for the left foot." He laughed. "Can't tell the difference, eh?"

"Sure I can." She pulled them on and got to her feet. Her red pants and yellow shirt were both filthy dirty.

"I'll wash your pants and shirt when we get to the spring. There's yucca plants there we can use for soap. Take your canvas bag around and find some shade if there is any. First drink some water. All you want. Never do without water in the desert unless you have to. You can keel over and if there's nobody around you could kick the bucket. Go ahead."

She drank from a gourd and said, "I can help you tote things."

He looked at her. Her face was so dirty he couldn't see the freckles. "Sure you can, honey. Tote the water gourds."

The burros had already moved off to find shade on the east side of the nearby saguaro. The tall cactus was casting a shadow only about four feet long, and both burros were trying to get in that little shade. Later they would stand nose to tail, in line behind the cactus, using all of the shade. They were smart little beasts, but not smart enough for each to choose a saguaro to stand behind. It never failed to tickle Kestrel.

When they had everything moved to the east side of the ironwood tree, Kestrel built another fire and made tortillas to go with the beans. After he'd eaten his fill, he said, "Now I'll get me some sleep, honey. If you're awake just before sundown, wake me up and we'll watch for doves. Okay?"

"Okay."

So he cleared a spot in the shade and lay down, a little concerned that he might oversleep and miss the evening doves. If he did, they'd have to stay put another night and day. It occurred to him that the girl was big enough to have good sense and that she was now his partner, and as such she had certain responsibilities. He slept.

The hot dry smell of the midday heat settled around her. All was still and quiet as the desert baked under the torturing sun. From behind her came the soft rustle of a lizard beneath the ironwood tree. The shadow in which she sat reached out to just beyond her new moccasins. Her skin and the top of her head felt dry and hot. She licked her lips and almost before her tongue went back into her mouth her lips were dry again.

Bits and pieces of thoughts kept darting around inside her head. The brown pony with the white spots and three white stockings. Did ponies really wear stockings? Did Mr. Hannibal really fetch her new pony, and was Henry the hired hand tending it the way she would tend it? Papa. He liked being called Papa instead of Daddy. Did Papa remember to get the saddle for the pony? The boy called Joe. Was he pouring water on another girl's head. Gila woodpecker. Did the bats leave the woodpecker's nesting hole in the saguaro tree when the woodpecker returned? She stirred and drew her legs up on the canvas bag. Her feet itched inside her new moccasins. Thirsty again. She reached for one of the water gourds piled beside her and worried the stopper out of the neck. Ahhaaa! Was water always this good and cool and she didn't know it? The stopper is cactus pulp, Mr. Kestrel had told her. He's a nice man, not like those old badmen at all.

Waves of superheated air pressed in around her. It reminded her of the stove at home when Hazel the hired girl was baking bread and opened the oven door and the dry heat came out to flood the kitchen with a wave of hot smelly goodness. She tilted the gourd and swallowed, spilling drops of icy coldness down her chin onto her shirt front. Ahaaa! How cool and nice. She remembered the feel of the water when the boy called Joe spilled water on her head. Shivery, "Next time don't be so damn stubborn." Mama called her that sometimes. "You can't always have what you want, Libby Wakefield. And what you want is not always best for you." Daddy never said that to her. Daddy was better than Mama. She loved Daddy best. She drank again and spilled some on her red pants to feel the icy coolness. How quickly it dries. More. How quick! One, two, three, four—gone! The rising vapor cooled her face.

Hawk. That's a redtail hawk up there. Pretty bird, the hawk. She liked the Gila woodpecker best. Funny bird. She raised the gourd and let a few drops drip on her head. How delicious. More. She poured it on, catching her breath. The gourd was empty. She put the stopper back in the neck the way Mr. Kestrel showed her. Cactus pulp. Funny man. No pants like other men, only a flap in front and back. She turned her head and looked at him, asleep with his mouth open. Would he jump if she poured water on him? Better not. She reached for another gourd but the stopper was too far down in the neck so she put it aside and took another and the stopper came out easy. She drank and poured what was left on her head. Wonderful. How quickly it dries. One, two, three, four, five, six—gone!

She reached for another gourd. "Drink all you want. We've got plenty." She drank and poured the rest on her head.

Kestrel squirmed in his sleep, trying to draw away from his dehydrated body. The hut was on fire. Crawl out the door, quick! Snipe. Wake up! Help me! I can't crawl!

He came awake with a jerk and saw at once that it was late. The girl was sitting on her canvas bag holding a gourd in her lap. He got to his feet and looked around at the sky. The sun was almost gone, another ten minutes. He looked at the girl again and saw that her eyes were closed as though in a trance.

"Honey."

Her eyelids fluttered open and she looked up at him. "Hi, Mr. Kestrel. You make awful noises when you sleep."

He tried to speak again but his mouth was too dry. He bent over to pick up a gourd. It was empty. He chose another. Empty too.

"Here." The girl held up the gourd she was holding in her lap. He took it and drank until it was empty. He gave it back to her and said, "Doves."

"Oh! I forgot!"

"That's all right, honey. Maybe there's time yet." He searched the air above the desert plants in all directions. He saw a pair and followed their flight, making a mental note of their direction. "Help me look, honey. Point out any you see." He made a full turn, noting that the sun was fast sinking. Come on, birds. There! He followed two more. Same direction. He took five seconds to find the spear and lay it on the ground to mark the course of the last pair of doves. Come on birds.

"There's two!"

"Where?"

"There." The girl pointed and he saw them at once. Two seconds and they were out of sight. The birds were flying low, just above the tops of the desert plants, as doves so often do. They were upon them and gone in seconds.

"There's two!"

He saw them at the same time. Same direction. Coming a little more from the west of south. He adjusted the spear a few inches.

"Keep looking."

The sun dropped down behind the horizon but still the birds were flying. He kept looking until it grew too gray to see the birds. He looked down at the spear and then in the direction the birds had come from. A little west of south. "Don't touch the spear, honey. Don't even get near it. When the stars come out we'll set our course by it. If we move the spear we'll never be able to set a true course."

"I won't touch it. I promise."

Long years of habit and deeply ingrained caution prompted him to look around for the burros. They were browsing over to the east. In the fast-fading light he could just barely make them out. He next checked the gear lying around on the ground. Something instantly clicked in his head and a slight tingling ran up his backbone. All of the gourds were out of the packs and scattered around the canvas bag the girl had been sitting on. He bent over to pick up a dozen gourds in succession. All were empty. He grew momentarily frantic and scrambled around looking for gourds with water. He found three. The other ninety-four were empty. But they'd used less than half! He refused to believe it and lifted and shook every gourd—still only three full ones. With his lips curling back in a sickly grin he looked at the girl.

She seemed to sense that she'd done wrong. "You told me we had plenty." It was not a whine; it was a simple statement of fact.

He straightened up and took a minute to compose himself. "Yes," he croaked and licked his parched lips. "Yes. It's all right, honey." He stared at the spear and gazed off at the twilit horizon. Please God, let the doves be right, he prayed. He picked up the three full gourds and held them against his chest. They were all that lay between them and certain disaster. Less, for these three belonged to the burros. No. The burros could subsist on the juices of desert succulents. He stood paralyzed for a time, and then his reason slowly came back to him. What was he so frightened about? They could hold on for one more day. Longer if they found a dry wash where healthy trees lived. But there were no washes in this area of no hills. All right, barrel cactus then. He took heart and turned to the girl.

"Honey, from now on we're partners. And being a partner in the desert means you looking out for me and me looking out for you. We don't do a thing without first telling each other. It may not be important, but like the water gourds it might mean the difference between living and dying. Do you understand that much so far?"

"I think I do."

"Well, you must be certain that you do, honey. When I say 'something,' I don't mean the usual things we do, like me fixing something to eat or you helping me load the girls. But anything that is not usual we must tell each other before we do them. Now do you understand?"

"Yes."

"From now on I'm going to explain everything to you. Why and how and everything. And if there's something you want to know about or something you don't understand, you must ask. It is your duty to ask."

"All right."

He drew a deep breath and looked in the direction the spear was pointing. There were stars showing, but none as yet around the horizon to the south. He needed a star to head toward. Was the spear pointing in the absolutely correct direction? Bull Quartz Spring was not a big place.

They could easily miss it in the moonlight. How far? He could only guess. It could be anywhere between two and twenty miles away. Doves rarely lived farther than twenty miles from water. What should he do? Go five miles and stop to wait for daylight when he could see? Was five miles far enough? Too far? Suppose they passed the hill of white rocks in the night? What then? Go on to Ironwood Hill and the Papagos? Too far. They would never—but why not? The reed would save them. He fought off a wave of despair.

Reaction set in. "What in the devil did you do with all the water, for heaven's sake?!"

The little girl drew back and stood there, frightened at his harsh tone of voice. Her face began to crumple and her eyelids fluttered. "I—" and she stopped.

He realized his mistake. "Sorry, honey. It doesn't matter now. The water's gone. Forgive me for shouting at you. Now let's eat something and get everything packed and call the girls in. Watch the spear!" He leaped and seized her arm just in time. Then from an overwhelming flood of emotion he pulled her close and hung on with desperation. She let him hold her until at last he let go and stepped back. "Sorry," he muttered, and looked around as if he'd lost something. "Let's eat now."

The girl picked up the three full gourds he'd been holding and set them with care on her sitting pallet. She then made an effort to redeem herself by fussing around packing the empty gourds in the bags.

Kestrel pulled himself together and became his usual efficient self again. He built a fire, used some of the precious water to mix batter for a corn cake, and put it on to bake in the big skillet. He warmed the tepary beans even though the air was still close to frying temperature, and when the hoecake was baked, they ate.

"Are you thirsty now?" he asked her.

"No."

"Don't say no when you mean yes, please. The three gourds full will last us all night. No sense saving water when we'll have all we need when we get to Bull Quartz Spring. Here. Drink."

She took the gourd and drank greedily. The air was so hot, with just a hint of the coolness of night coming on. When she handed back the gourd he pretended to drink and then pushed the stopper into the neck. Water had never been so precious. He still couldn't imagine what she had done with over forty gourds full of water. It boggled his mind.

He got up and looked at the horizon in the direction the spear pointed. There was a star, but he knew that all stars with the exception of the North Star moved as the earth turned; that star he was looking at now might by midnight be way over to the west. Yet he still needed something to head towards. He went around the spear and checked the way it was lined up in relation to the North Star. It pointed about one fingerwidth to the east. He committed that to memory. One fingerwidth was the space taken up by one finger held up six inches in front of his eyes. He and Snipe used the method and it seemed to work.

When everything was packed and ready to load, he called in the burros, giving silent thanks that they were so tame and gentle and such pets. This would be a bad time to have to go hunting burros the way so many prospectors did. The burros came in after a while, as they always did, taking their time about it. He put on their halters and then the packsaddles and tied down the canvas bags. When ready, he lit a piece of cactus wood in the fire and looked around to make sure he wasn't forgetting something.

"You ride, honey. I'll be too busy keeping us on course and doing a lot of hard thinking to watch over you. Up!" He lifted her up and set her on the dominant burro.

The last thing he did was pick up the spear, hating to do it even then. He started off and kept as straight a course as he could manage for about a mile. The compacted forest of desert growth began to thin out. He and the girl were in a situation that called for clear thinking and good judgment, and to do that he had to tax his brain. He thought hard, taking a look at every possibility, and decided that it would be smart not to travel just in a straight line but to cover a wider swath of territory by zigzagging, weaving his way to the west and then back toward the east a mile or so each way, counting the steps. He decided on one thousand steps to begin with, then back two thousand steps and two thousand each way after that.

"Can you count to a thousand, honey?"

"I can count to a hundred."

"Never mind." He went on to explain to her what he intended to do.

The night air cooled and the moon came up. From a slow walk he increased their pace to just short of a trot. The area was beginning to look more promising, more like the area around the spring that he remembered. Bur sage and creosote bush. He took heart. Now he could see a good distance toward the west and about half the distance toward the east, looking into the moon's dim glare. He continued to zigzag, and as he got farther along, he closed the zigs and zags so as not to chance missing the big white rocks and leaving them behind in one of the half loops. By midnight he was going three thousand steps to his right and three thousand to his left, taking in a larger and larger area. Several times he was tempted to straighten his course and firmly resisted the temptation.

And all the while he talked with the girl. Explaining endlessly. He told her what he was doing, why, and how. He vowed never again to take anything for granted with her. Had he explained to her that water was precious and had to be used sparingly, she would not have used the water. He was sure of that; she was a smart little girl. He told her stories about happenings to him and Snipe over the past six years. She asked sensible questions and he answered them all fully.

Once she said, "Daddy and Mama never tell me anything I want to know. I'm supposed to know already."

"That's too often the way of parents, honey," he said. "They think, or don't think is better, that just because they know something then you're supposed to know it too. My dad and mom were that way. The only one around the farm who ever explained things to me and Snipe was old William. He was Snipe's dad. A great man, old William was."

Long after midnight, when it seemed to him that he had zigged and zagged a hundred times, he jumped a deer. He stopped right there, unloaded the burros, and settled down to wait for daylight. Deer would not go far from their watering place. With the first break of day the doves began calling, and soon he saw them flying off toward the northwest. He'd passed it!

He looked in that direction but could not see anything that could be the white hill of Bull Quartz Spring. About twenty minutes after he saw the first doves leaving the area he saw the first ones coming back. Five to ten miles, more or less, he reasoned. He didn't wait. Already the sun was up and they were completely out of water. He was very thirsty, and even though the girl had had water during the night, twice what he had drunk, he knew she must be very thirsty too.

It was no longer a gamble; he was certain that there was water off in that direction, so he went with a light heart. But five miles in the hot sun was a long way. The burros grew testy. The little girl got listless. And he was on the brink of going heat crazy when at last he saw in the distance the shining white boulders and the top of a fan palm tree.

It was not a mirage.

CHAPTER FOURTEEN

The sun was almost directly overhead when Joe Brown saw up ahead the three-armed saguaro and the white rag. He was about dead on his feet. He had been without water since midnight. The others, strung out behind him, six on horses and two on foot bringing up the drag, were footsore and delirious with the heat and their thirst. The six horses were in better condition than the men. Hobart and Kelly were the two on drag. It was against Hobart's principles to ride when even one of his men had to walk.

Hobart had just about reached the end of his strength, and he knew it. He'd been walking spraddle-legged for the past three or four miles and he had the feeling that he'd topple over just any second now. When he heard Joe Brown calling in a dry, croaking voice that he'd found the campsite, Hobart could scarcely give it a care. He staggered on, and when he reached the shade where the others were frantically digging for the water kegs, the best he could do was collapse.

By a strange phenomenon, during the next hour none of the men ever actually noticed the message stuck to the saguaro, although they all saw it. Their minds rejected what their eyes were seeing.

After digging a hole deep enough to bury a horse, it was the old man Forty Acre Smith who said what everybody else refused to believe. "They ain't here, men. The polecat done beat us to 'em." He drew back from the circle of diggers that looked like a crap game in session and plopped down beside Hobart. "They done us in, sergeant. That grinning galoot and his sidekick's got us licked."

"You figured they would, didn't you?" Hobart felt sore all over, and his feet inside his boots were being roasted alive. "How far do you reckon it is to that spring from here?"

"This is as far as any of us is ever going to get, Jason." Forty hadn't called Hobart by his first name more than once or twice. It was as if he was making a belated offer of friendship. "I'm so dry my blood's thick as pine pitch."

"You'll feel better once you cool off a bit." Hobart looked at the others. Blount looked as if he'd lost fifty pounds. Magpie and Moss were racks of bones with skulls for heads. Stump Brown had rolled a smoke and didn't have enough spit to lick it into shape. Only Joe Brown and the cowhands Kelly and Jerome looked like they might live another hour. The rest of us is done for, he thought. "Bloody runt bastard."

"I just can't figure it, Forty." He had to mold each word into shape before he could breathe it out. "Two men and one of 'em a runt no bigger than a twelve-year-old boy. Maybe not even two men. We never did get a good look. And you know what blows my bugle? We ain't never going to spend a penny of our gold. Not one red copper.

That runt booger's out there someplace right this minute. Maybe right back of that overgrown fence post. He'll wait for us to croak plum dead. I'm mighty tired, Forty. Reckon I'll get me a bit of sleep." He let himself topple over sideways and lay there sucking in hot air.

A few minutes later Forty Acre Smith lay back and closed his eyes. He could feel his heart pounding with big, blasting thumps as if it was trying to force molasses through a clogged pipe.

Gower Blount pulled himself over to where Moss was sitting and held out his last cigar. "Have yourself a good smoke, Moss," he said, and Moss got down on his hands and knees and slowly crawled away.

The three boys were the only ones who sought company in their misery. They sat together in silence like three lost pups.

The last words any of them spoke were from Joe Brown. "We never should of took that little girl, Kelly."

Kelly didn't respond. They all sat around with their eyes closed against the glare of the sun, and an hour later they all drifted off into coma.

From the slope of Black Hill Two Snipe saw the bandits when they were still four miles from the campsite. He could make out six horses with riders and three men on foot. He had found a spot on the shady side of a saguaro that gave him a clear view of the campsite and the white rag. He followed the bandits as they made their way and saw them digging frantically. After a while the horses wandered around and settled for shade and rest before doing any foraging. They still wore their saddles.

He waited for an hour by the sun, and when he saw no more activity, he guessed that when the men had found the kegs missing, they had collapsed exhausted or had opted to rest. The white rag did not come down. He strained his eyes and thought he saw the message still impaled to the saguaro with the arrow.

When the sun got directly overhead and there was no more shade, he worked his way down the slope and headed toward the bandits. With all his caution he worked his way across the flat, always keeping some bush or tree between himself and the campsite. A bobcat stalking a wild turkey couldn't have gone any slower. As he made his way closer to the camp, he spotted two of the horses. They had sought shelter from the sun on the east side of a mesquite tree, but there wasn't much shade now at midday. He inspected them and decided that they were in better shape than they had any right to be. Hardy little beast, the mustang. They deserved better treatment than they'd got from the bandits.

He began circling the campsite at a good distance, searching for a clear field of vision. He found it after he'd crossed the trail on the north side. The message was still stuck to the saguaro. He saw men lying on the ground. Two were lying in the sun. He counted nine altogether.

After ten more minutes, when not one of the nine men moved so much as a finger, he went closer. This was the sticky moment. Should just one of them rise up and spot him, he could be killed with one shot. He didn't like taking such a risk. It wasn't his way of doing things. But after some consideration he decided that this time the game just might be worth the candle. So he moved forward, keeping a bush or cactus clump between himself and the bandits, ready at the first sign of a finger flick to run like hell. Once or twice he stopped and watched the men for a long time. None moved. They could very well be dead. But he'd heard of presumably dead soldiers on battlefields who became very much alive and deadly.

From behind a cholla cactus tree twenty feet from the nearest man he observed them, and when none moved after another ten minutes, he eased around the cholla and went forward quickly. He snatched up a Winchester '73 rifle and made sure it was fully loaded. He cocked the hammer behind a shell and kept a wary eye on the men as he slowly made the rounds gathering up their guns. When he had them all in a pile fifty yards away he scraped out a long trench about a foot deep and buried the guns.

His spirits rose when he went back to look for the money. It was not on the men themselves. He took down the message and arrow and went looking for the horses. The first one he found had, among other gear, two saddlebags, each of which held about ten pounds of gold coins. He ran the coins through his fingers the way all men do at such times and gloated, if only for a few seconds. He slung the saddlebags over one of the horses and taking the reins he went to round up the others. One and two at a time he took the horses east of the camp and tied them in the shade of an ironwood tree. They were carrying nine pairs of saddlebags in all. He searched out shells for the Winchester and put them in with the gold in one saddlebag, then put all nine saddlebags on one horse, the best horse of the lot. He chose the second best horse to ride. He unsaddled the other four horses and took off their bridles and gave them slaps on their rumps. They didn't run off, they walked.

With the rifle still cocked, he went back to the campsite. The bandits were still unconscious. He counted them to make sure one hadn't woke up and was up to mischief.

When he was sure they were not playing dead, he went to where he'd reburied one keg and dug it up. Then he went around and scratched the sand off the other three kegs so they could be seen. He rolled the one keg over to the two horses, stood it up, and used the rifle butt to bash in the end. He let the two horses drink their fill and then filled his six water gourds.

When he had everything ready for a quick getaway, he took the rifle back to the men and looked them over. He chose a young boy with a smooth face and poked him a few times to make sure he wasn't dogging it. He wasn't. He was still alive, if barely.

Taking hold of the boy's arm, he dragged him to the opened ten-gallon keg by the horses. He didn't try to be gentle. He set the boy up, spread his legs apart, put the keg between his legs, and held his head over the opening. "Water, kid! Water! Drink!" It was useless. So he put down the rifle reluctantly and used one hand to hold the boy up while he sloshed water with the other hand. He had to keep it up for all of ten minutes before the boy stirred and opened his eyes. "Water! Drink, you idiot!" He pushed the boy's head down into the keg.

The boy got the message. He wrapped his arms around the keg and sucked up the water like a barnyard pump. Snipe kept asking him if he was all right and after a long time the boy came up for air and managed a cracked-lip "Much oblige."

"Look at me," Snipe commanded, and when the boy lifted his face and focused his eyes, Snipe said, "There's three more kegs of water in holes around the camp. About fifty or so yards out. You can find them easy enough. I've uncovered them. Can you fix up your friends if I leave you now?"

"Who're you?" the boy asked.

"My name is Snipe Morgan."

"But you're a darky."

"That's right, kid. There's a spring about eight miles south of here. You passed it on your way north. Remember it?"

"Sure. Hold it. I need some more of this." The boy called Kelly stuck his head back into the keg.

When he came up for air, Snipe said, "I'm leaving you now, kid. Your friends are all passed out. Get water to them, and when you're on your feet, I suggest you head for the spring. Do you understand that?"

"Sure. Go to the spring. Are you the guy's been dogging our asses the last fifty-odd miles?"

"That was me. Now you'd better get back to your friends and out of this sun. So long."

"Wait."

"Make it fast."

"Why did you wake me up?"

"I just don't like killing people. Does that cure your itch?"

"Yeah. I reckon it does. Well, much oblige, Snipe Morgan, is it?"

"That's right. Snipe Morgan. Black man. So long, kid." He pulled himself up in the saddle, took the reins of the gold-bearing mustang, and rode away.

Kelly watched the black man out of sight and stuck his head back into the keg. When the water in his belly felt like he'd swallowed a whole watermelon, he got to his feet and went back to the campsite.

"God, they're all dead," he muttered and went looking for the kegs the black man had said were uncovered. He found one, worried it out of the ground, and rolled it to the shade on the east side of the saguaro and paloverde tree. Standing it on end, he got the bung out and looked for something that would hold water. He found an empty canteen, filled it, and went to work on his friend Joe Brown.

After Joe came to, Kelly revived the others in accordance with how well he liked them. Joe first, then Jerome, Hobart, Forty Acre, Stump Brown, Magpie, and lastly Blount. Moss was dead. The eight of them consumed water as if it was raining the stuff. By the time Hobart had his wits about him and cut down on the consumption, they had one full keg and a piece of a second keg left. About eleven gallons in all.

By the middle of the afternoon they were all in fairly good condition except for the dead Moss. The near fatal disaster had taken a lot of the grit out of them all. They lay in the shade listlessly and suffered the heavy heat. All of them had cracked and swollen lips and talking was painful.

"You sure it wasn't no Indian?" Hobart asked Kelly for the tenth time.

"He was a darky and he talked good as you do. Maybe better. He wore Injun garb though. Couple of leather flaps and he had a band around his head like a Apache. Wore Injun shoes too."

"And you didn't get a look at the other feller?"

"There weren't no other feller."

"What makes you so sure there weren't no other feller?"

"I never seen none but the one feller and I seen him ride away. He rode off on my horse. Had Jerome's horse in tow with the gold in our saddlebags. There weren't nobody but the darky."

"Well, it don't matter none how many there was," Hobart said, accepting the apparent fact that one man had bested them all. "There was two of them took away the little girl though. Ain't that right, Forty?"

Before Forty could respond, Blount threw up his hands and yelled at Hobart. "Stop kicking the damn dog! He's dead, for chrissake. One man or fifty. What's the bloody difference? He's gone. Took off with all our money. Gone! You hear me." He collapsed for lack of air to go on with.

Hobart got to his feet and stood over Blount like a bantam rooster over a grub worm. "On your feet, Blount. I'm gonna peel the hide off your rotten carcass. Up!"

"Aw, lay off, Jason," Forty Acre Smith said from a reclining position. "He ain't worth kicking out the door. We gotta start thinking about getting to where there's some water."

Hobart subsided. Forty was right. There was enough water in the kegs to last through the day and the coming night and that was all. He sat back down and worried his boots off his aching feet. "I ain't used to walking," he complained.

Forty said, "You ain't the only galoot what ain't, Jason. But we got us a lot of walking yet. Eight, maybe ten more miles. Be a hundred before we get there. I get sore every time I think about it."

Hobart sacrificed a dribble of water from his canteen to cool his feet. "If I had me a gun and a horse, I'd go after that runt. Whack his bygod gonads off."

Magpie cleared his throat and said in a singsong voice, "If wishes were horses then beggars would ride, and if horseshit was biscuits we'd eat till we died."

"Aw, shut up, you old goat."

Magpie cackled. "Trouble with you geezers is you don't know how to laugh. It's a joke! The whole bygod world is a big fat joke."

Old Stump Brown looked around at the baking desert and said, "How can anybody stay alive out here in this short-grass country beats hell up to me."

"You gotta be a thief to do it, Stump," Magpie said. "Like that feller what stole our teeth right outta our heads."

Hobart said, "You gotta admire a man like that, once you think on it. There we was with horses and guns. A bloody army, for chrissake. He was on foot and I bet he didn't even have a pepperbox pistol. Nothing but a bow and arrows like a bygod redskin, and he licked us all to who laid the chunk. Like to meet up with him someday. I'd buy him a drink."

"Yeah. Me too," Magpie said. "Well, sergeant. Do we

walk come dark or do we squat here till the buzzards get at us?"

"We walk. Least I do. I ain't dead yet. Come sundown I'm heading for that spring. I'm needing me a wash all over. Ain't had me a all-over wash for nigh on to a year. Think of that, men. All the water you can drink and some to throw away. Who's going with me?"

"Count us in, sergeant," Joe Brown said for himself and Kelly and Jerome.

"Forty?"

"I'll give it a go."

"Magpie?"

"I'll go far as I can make it. Can't ask a man for more than that."

"Stump?"

"What the hell for? Might as well kick the bucket here as there. Same difference, way I see it. Once we get to that spring, we'll be stuck right there till old Pete toots his bugle."

"Maybe so, old timer," Hobart said. "We can just about figure that runt's gone to dig up the kegs south of the spring. Onery bastard. All right then. It's settled. Come sundown we go. Fill your canteens to take along and we'll drink what's left before we pull out. After we get to the spring, we can figure out how to get out of this hellhole." He didn't bother to ask Blount to join them. He didn't care what happened to him.

"We going to plant old Moss?" Forty asked.

"Naw. He won't mind feeding the buzzards. He was scared of ghosts. Did you know that?"

"Ghosts can't hurt a body," Magpie said. "All they do is help you slit your own throat."

"Yeah. Like that desert ghost what did us in, eh?"

"The desert ghost," Stump mulled, looking around as if one might be present.

At first dark they all started off, including Stump, and by walking all night, driven on by Hobart, they got to One Palm Spring the next morning an hour after sunup.

As they collapsed under the saguaro-rib shelter after filling their bellies with water at the spring, Hobart said, "Well, we bygod made it. Now you ain't about to get me away from here till I settle the score with that bloody runt."

"I'm taking out me a homestead on this spot," Forty Acre Smith said. "Raise me some of them camels they got down to Arizona Territory. Be big money in camels."

The others laughed. They were safe. The long ordeal was over.

After he left the bandit kid to tend to his cohorts, Snipe rode west about three miles and stopped in the shade of a joshua tree. He wasn't worried about the bandits chasing after him, not on foot in the shape they were in, but he thought it best to put a little distance between himself and them just in case. Taking unnecessary risks was not his way of doing things.

Unsaddling the two horses, he hobbled them both and turned them loose to forage or sleep in the shade. He knew that he would have to forage for them soon. Burros could feed themselves on the desert foliage, but horses not accustomed to feeding on cactus plants and spiny mesquite foliage could go hungry.

Pulling the nine saddlebags into the shade, he spread one of the saddle pads and dumped the gold coins in a pile. It made a lovely sight. He found the poke that the bandits had taken from them in the bank and put it aside. They would need the poke when they took the girl to Prospect.

He separated the coins according to denomination. The fifty-dollar gold slugs in one pile, the twenty-dollar double eagles in another, the ten-dollar eagles in a pile to themselves, the five-dollar half eagles in one pile, the two-and-one-half-dollar coins in one pile, and the one-dollar gold coins by their little old selves. There were some silver coins and some coppers. Those he all but scorned. The bank notes he stacked up and weighted down with a rock.

The tablet and pencil stub came in handy again. He listed each size coin separately, and when he got through counting the lovely stuff the total looked something like this:

27 fifty-dollar gold slugs
626 double eagles
724 eagles
685 half eagles
129 two-and-one-half-dollar gold pieces
419 one-dollar gold pieces
$1742.00 in bank notes

The silver he didn't bother to count. The copper cents he tossed away as not worth toting.

When he had the final tally to show Kestrel, he put the

whole pile of gold coins into one pair of saddlebags. It weighed a hefty ninety pounds or better. On second thought, he opted for two pairs of saddlebags. They'd need two pairs of saddlebags in any case when they split it up. Besides, so much weight might bust a leather bag and he surely didn't want that to happen. There'd be gold coins strung out all the way to Bull Quartz Spring. For a long time he sat on the ground in the shade admiring the bulging saddlebags; then he got up and went in search of a barrel cactus for the horses.

Between sundown and dark he used the Winchester to shoot a jackrabbit for his supper. He was almost as pleased with the rifle as he was with the gold. Here in the desert a gun was often more valuable than any amount of gold, to his notion. Not that he would trade the gold for a rifle, now or ever. He'd make do with his bow and spears first.

While the rabbit roasted, he brought in the horses and tied them to a nearby mesquite. Then he leisurely ate the rabbit and waited for the moon to come up. Bull Quartz Spring was only about another seven miles away, to the west. He could walk the horses that far in two or three hours.

While waiting for the moon, he laid out a plan for the return of the little girl to her father. It wouldn't do to let the girl know that he had her father's money, so he would bury it near Bull Quartz Hill before seeing her and Kestrel. He would take it easy for two or three days to rest the horses. No, that wouldn't do. He'd turn the horses loose and go in on foot. No. He couldn't tote ninety pounds of gold. He'd have to sneak in on the east side of

Bull Quartz Hill, bury the gold, take the horses back out on the flat, turn them loose, and then go in on foot. That was better. Then he'd rest up for a few days and walk to Prospect with Kestrel and the burros and the girl. No, not two or three days of rest. What for? He wasn't tired. The gold had marvelous qualities for pepping a man up.

What story would he tell the banker and the town marshal? The truth up to the time he took the girl away from the bandits, because the girl knew about all that. Then he'd say he followed the bandits as far as One Palm Spring. That's all. Keep it simple.

Why did you follow them, Mr. Morgan?

They would surely ask that question. The poke? He followed the bandits to see if he could get the poke back but couldn't. How could he? The only weapons he had was a bow and two spears. What made you think you could get the poke back, Mr. Morgan? Well, he'd crept into the bandits' camp to take the girl, hadn't he? He figured he could get the poke back the same way he'd taken the girl, but the bandits were too alert at night after losing the girl.

He went over the plan and saw a few weak spots. Why did you go after the bandits in the first place, Mr. Morgan? Was to get the poke back the only reason?

He gnawed on that meatless bone for a time. Reward? But how did you know there was a reward, Mr. Morgan? Was a reward offer so reasonable that he took it for granted? That could well be the case. And the important thing was the fact that he and Kestrel were desert men. Who other than desert men could better take the girl back?

Aw, come on now, Mr. Morgan. Are you seriously asking us to believe you tackled nine bandits with nothing more than a bow and two spears? No, sir. All we accomplished was taking the girl away from them. We didn't kill any bandits. There was no fight.

Would the banker and town marshal buy that story? They would not. It was too obvious that he and Kestrel had gone after the bandits for the sole purpose of taking the gold and making away with it like a pair of thieves. Very well. Say as much to begin with. Admit that they had been after the gold. So they rescued the little girl first and, after that, they were unable to take the gold. The bandits were too many and too alert and well armed. Stick to the truth. All but the gold. The bandits got away with the gold.

That was it. He and Kestrel had disobeyed the law by going after the bandits after being told not to go. Was that a crime? If so it was a very little one. Worthy of a five-dollar fine at most. They could afford five dollars, couldn't they? Snipe laughed at a cactus wren that had come to investigate who was sitting under its foraging tree.

He asked himself more potential questions. Where did you get the poke of gold you have now, Mr. Morgan? The answer to that was not to take the poke of gold to Prospect. They wouldn't need it. Surely the banker would pay them some kind of reward for returning his darling daughter. Leave the poke buried with the loot.

Any more questions?

He went through the whole story again. "Sir, we saw the bandits take the gold. So when they rode south into the desert, we went after them, hoping to take the gold away from them. The second night out we were able to rescue the girl. Kestrel took the girl to a safe place while I followed the bandits to get the gold. That proved impossible, so I gave up and went to the safe place and we came on back here."

Was that reasonable enough? Was it believable? The only thing he had actually achieved had been the rescue of the girl. The rest of the story was just about what any two unarmed men could have done.

By the time the moon came up, he was satisfied that the story would hold up. He saddled the horses, lifted up the two saddlebags and made them doubly fast to the saddle, and mounted the other horse.

He moved out, setting a course for Bull Quartz Spring. Two hours later, as the eastern sky was just beginning to show light, he arrived at the east side of Bull Quartz Hill. The palms and spring were on the other side.

The hill, rising out of the flat desert and covering perhaps ten acres, was like no other hill he had seen during his rambles with Kestrel. Smooth white boulders, some small, some huge, were piled on top of each other like gigantic eggs laid by a giant bird. Around the edge a dense forest of desert plants lived, taking moisture from under the boulders and giving the whole affair the look of a bird's nest of enormous size.

Where did the water come from? The Papagos had told them that long ago a great god stopped here to rest and struck the rocks to bring forth water to quench his thirst. The water was sweet and pure and delightfully refreshing to drink. After long hours of speculation, he and Kestrel had agreed that the water probably was fossil water that had been trapped underground for many years, perhaps for hundreds of years.

Snipe selected a spot between two small boulders, each the size of a covered wagon, a spot easily recognizable and easy to describe that he would never forget, and buried the saddlebags between them. That done, he took the horses back out on the flat desert of creosote bush and bur sage and unsaddled them before turning them loose. He knew that they would go to the spring to drink, and they would probably remain around the white hill for months, until some passing Indian or prospector found them.

He slung the pack on his back and was bending over to pick up the spears and rifle when he paused. He could not safely take the Winchester. He could not explain with any satisfaction how he got it. So he left it with the saddles and bridles under a creosote bush. He would retrieve the rifle when he returned with Kestrel to retrieve the banker's gold.

The sun was well up when he rounded the north side of the hill and saw Kestrel and the girl about a hundred yards down the west side. They were camped under a stand of fan palms a good distance from the spring. No desert man ever camps right next to a spring. It is the worst sin he can commit. The birds and animals were there first.

The palms, covering perhaps two acres in competition with a dense growth of joshua trees, ironwood trees, cottonwoods, and a score of other kinds of trees and bushes, including a wild lemon tree whose seed had come from only God knew where, made him feel cool just looking at it. The area, including the hill, was a haven for just about every animal and bird that calls the desert home. Mountain lions lived up in the rocks and preyed on mule deer, javalina pig, jackrabbits, ground squirrels, and chulas, among others. A bevy of over a thousand desert quail lived in the area and around it. Doves came from twenty miles in all directions to drink at the spring. Snipe had camped here with Kestrel and the burros a dozen times or more, often months at a time. It was a desert oasis in the most meaningful sense of the word.

As he walked toward them, Kestrel spotted him and called out, "Hey!" His face blossomed in a sparkling smile. He stood there with the girl, aglow with happiness to see him. When Snipe drew close, Kestrel came forward and they embraced like long-parted lovers, their arms around each other, patting each other on the back.

When Snipe drew back, still holding onto Kestrel's arms, he said, "How goes it, Kes?"

"Just great. You?"

For the girl's benefit Snipe said, "I followed them as far as One Palm Spring. I didn't get a chance to get our poke back. Too many men with too many guns." He winked one eye and turned to the girl. "And how have you been, Miss Libby?"

The girl beamed at him. "Just fine, Mr. Snipe. We've had loads of fun. We trapped some quail yesterday and early this morning Mr. Kestrel speared a wild pig. That's it there."

The naked body of a javalina pig was spitted on a stick above the fire, roasting.

"I could eat half of that myself," Snipe said, sniffing the aroma. "How long have you been here, Kes?"

"Since yesterday morning."

"We got lost," the girl said.

Kestrel grinned and lifted an eyebrow at his partner. "It sounds more romantic to put it that way. We weren't lost, but we had a close call. Tell you all about it later. Could you eat now? I can whack off some of the pig and fry it."

"I can wait. Miss Libby, suppose you tend to the pig while we go off and talk partner talk. Okay?"

"I'm Mr. Kestrel's partner now too, Mr. Snipe."

"Indeed you are," Snipe told her. "But this is special man talk. Let's go down to the spring, Kes. I can use a drink of really good water."

The girl frowned her displeasure, but Snipe didn't care. She was a liability now. Without her they could pack up and head for Santa Fe, rich as fools.

They walked together on a game trail under the palms to the spring, flushing animals and birds to the right and left. Chulas peered down from the palms at them. The spring was a good producer. The ground for a hundred yards in three directions stayed moist. It was cool around the spring under the palms.

"I got it, Kes. Over twenty-five thousand in gold. Some bank notes and silver but mostly all gold. It's a sight to see. I buried it between two wagon-size boulders on the other side of the hill."

"Hot ziggidy!" Kestrel pounded one palm with a fist. "Have any trouble?"

"None to speak of."

"Are the bandits all at the place?"

"I didn't kill any. And I didn't follow them that far. But that's our story. Let me tell you all of it, then we'll agree on a story to tell the banker and the marshal." He went on to relate the story in full and in detail. Snipe was a natural-born storyteller. When he got through, Kestrel was grinning like a possum in a hen house.

"God!" he breathed. "I knew you could pull it off, Snipe. But still I was plenty worried. I hope you never have to go through anything like that again. Now, what is the story we tell the girl's dad and the marshal?"

"Well, old partner, I gave it a lot of hard thinking and this is what I came up with. 'Sir, we were in the bank and saw the bandits take the gold and we sort of got carried away. Greedy, you know. Like everybody else. Anyway, when they rode south into the desert we went after them, hoping to take the gold away from them for ourselves. No, we did not intend to bring it back. Do you take us for fools? In any event, the second night out we were able to rescue the girl. Kestrel took the girl to a safe place while I followed the bandits to get the gold away from them. That proved impossible, so I gave up and went to the safe place and from there we came right back here with the little girl.' How does that strike you?"

"Sounds convincing to me. We can make it stick tighter by asking the banker for that loan again."

"He doesn't have any money to lend, Kes. We've got it all."

"That doesn't matter. We'll ask for the loan anyway. He doesn't know we've got it." Kestrel paused for a moment and frowned while scrubbing his now quarter-inch-long whiskers. "You know," he said. "I sort of feel sorry for the man, Snipe."

"Don't you dare! Dammit, partner! He's the kind of man who can't help making money. He'll earn a hundred times more in a lifetime than we ever will. Let's just figure we earned it getting his daughter back to him. If you start having a guilty conscience, we'll never enjoy the damn money."

Kestrel grinned. "You've convinced me, mister. And we really did earn it, didn't we?"

"You bet your white ass we did, buddy."

They stood there and grinned at each other like a pair of prospectors who had just found the mother lode.

"How soon do you want to leave for Prospect?" Kestrel asked.

"Sundown suits me. How about you?"

"Suits me just fine. The girl's good company, but I'd far and away prefer yours. Let's go eat us some bygod pig. Damn shame we don't have any Mobile Bay oysters."

They laughed all the way to the campsite.

CHAPTER FIFTEEN

When Jack Shannon was hired as first deputy by Marshal Bill Butterworth the day after the bank robbery, he promptly organized the town kids into a group called The Prospect Scouts. The primary duty of the scouts was to report at once to Deputy Shannon any strangers entering the town from any direction, with a complete description plus, if possible, the stranger's name. The scouts group was an instant success because Shannon had the good sense to reward the kids. He kept a mason jar full of nickels and pennies in the marshal's office to pay the kids with. The first kid to report a stranger got a nickel; the next three kids to report the same stranger each got a penny. The competition among the kids was intense, for a nickel to a Prospect kid was a big hunk of money, and a penny wasn't to be kicked out of bed either.

The scouts made Jack Shannon's job as first deputy a snap. He was able through the use of his spies to keep an eye on everything that happened in Prospect, often before it happened. From first daylight until well after dark every day boys of eight to fourteen could be seen coming and going in and out of the town jail, which was located behind the Prospect Mercantile Store on North Valley Street. They entered bearing news and left bearing coins in their sweaty little paws. The coins were usually spent within minutes at the candy counters of the various stores along Main Street. A licorice bullwhip long as a boy's arm cost a penny. A nickel would buy a whole pound of assorted goodies.

The kids didn't just spy, they were outlaw hunters. They studied the wanted posters, memorized names and faces of badmen, and went about town wearing tin stars the local blacksmith turned out, peering at every face as if they were searching for lost uncles.

So it was that on Sunday morning, ten days after the bank robbery, a boy of nine called Peter Potts, who lived way out on South Valley Street, came bursting into the marshal's office to inform Deputy Shannon that he'd spotted two men, one black and one white, with two burros, and riding one of the burros was Libby Wakefield.

"And just where did you see all this, Peter me boy?" said Deputy Shannon as he paid Peter a nickel.

"Way out on South Valley, Deputy Jack, sir."

"Thank you, Peter. Now run tell Marshal Bill just what you told me." The boy shot out the door.

No sooner had the boy left than another boy came in with the same information, followed by four others. Shannon gave three of the five boys each a penny and told one to go fetch Mr. George Wakefield. They all ran out the door like a pack of Indians looking for a scalp to lift.

The scout spy system was functioning admirably.

Jack Shannon buckled on his gun belt, inspected the rounds in his Navy Colt, and swaggered out the door and down to the bank corner. The son of a miner, Jack wore walking boots, not riding boots. He didn't own a horse and wouldn't get up on one even if he did. When he walked he did so with a swagger. He swaggered out into the middle of the street the better to get an unobstructed view toward the south. Yes, there they were, a quarter mile away. He went to meet them, holding to the middle of the street.

It was early; the bank building on his left was casting a shadow clear across the fifty-foot-wide street of dusty adobe clay. As he went forward, he kept his eyes fixed on the two men and wondered why two bank robbers would see fit to fetch back the little girl. Proud of his ability to reason things out to a logical conclusion, he arrived at the probability that the two were unaware that the people of Prospect knew they were members of the Blount Gang. Still, even that didn't make much sense. If Blount had wanted to return the little girl, he could have put her aboard a stage someplace and forgot her. The Wells Fargo people would see to it that she was delivered safely into her father's arms.

Having progressed a hundred paces down the street, Deputy Shannon stopped and stood there spraddle-legged, the classic picture of the intrepid deputy town marshal confronting the local badman. He stood an inch over six feet, had shoulders a yard wide, and wore a facial expression guaranteed to cow the meanest of outlaws.

He waited, and when the two desert men drew to within fifty feet, he held up one hand and roared, "Hold it right there!"

The two men, both small, one black, one white, both

garbed in California pants and blue-cotton miner's shirts, stopped in their tracks and stood there staring at him with wonder on their faces.

The white man said, "Howdy, deputy. We're fetching the banker's daughter back to him."

The little girl, perched on a burro, called out to Deputy Shannon, "Hi, Mr. Jack!" and hopped off the burro as if she'd been doing it all her life. She landed on her feet as lightly as a bird and ran towards him while looking back over her shoulder at the two desert men.

Puzzled, Shannon looked around at the fast-gathering crowd and took the girl's hand as he went up to the two men. "You'll be explaining yourselves, I take it?"

The white man glanced sideways at the black man and said to the deputy, "We'd be damn fools if we didn't, deputy. It's simple enough. We rescued the little girl and we're fetching her back to her daddy. Where's the old marshal?"

"Marshal Bill will be right along, Mr. Morgan." The banker had told everybody about the two Morgans asking for a loan. Shannon looked down at the girl. "Did they hurt you, me lass?"

"Of course not. Mr. Kestrel and Mr. Snipe took me away from those nasty badmen. They're my partners." The little girl was perky as a roadrunner.

"Are they now?" Shannon said as he lifted an eyebrow.

"Lock 'em up, Jack!"

Shannon twisted his head to search the faces in the crowd and settled on the man who had shouted. He didn't say anything. He didn't have to. Even the toughest miners held respect for Jack Shannon's fists. He turned back to the two men. "You men will be coming along with me now," and executing a snappy about-face he swaggered off toward the bank corner and the jail. He found no need to look back. When Shannon told a man to do something, he did it. The girl danced along beside him, for like all the kids of the town she was very fond of the handsome Irishman. She knew she was the envy of every boy and girl tagging along. She had gone off adventuring with real live robbers and had been rescued and now knew everything there was to know about the desert. She would tell and retell the tale for years, elaborating until in the end the story had only a faint relationship with fact.

At the bank corner, where the town's two principle streets crossed, George Wakefield came running from out of the west. He snatched up his daughter and stood there trembling and weeping with joy and happiness. The crowd looked on with a collective feeling of shared pleasure.

"How touching."

"Poor old George."

When the banker put his daughter down after several minutes, he looked at the two prospectors, whom he still believed were members of the Blount Gang. "So Blount crossed you up, did he?" He seemed to take satisfaction from the fact. The fact as he saw it.

"Nobody crossed us up, mister," Kestrel told him, and shut his mouth when Snipe said, "Hold your temper, Kes."

The banker curled his lips and said to Jack Shannon, "Lock them up, deputy. On charges of bank robbery, assessory to triple murder, and child-taking."

Shannon stuck out his jaw. He was a born politician, but nobody pushed him around, even the town banker. "I can see no reason for that, Mr. Wakefield. They fetched back the wee girl of their own free will, sir, bless their hearts. We were wrong about them being kith and kin with the robbers."

Sharply, Wakefield said, "We'll decide that later, deputy. Where's Marshal Bill?"

Shannon turned to look up East Main Street and saw the old marshal hurrying toward them. While he was closing the distance, Snipe studied the faces in the crowd and read expressions of avid curiosity. Men, women, and kids, they waited expectantly to see a good show. Perhaps for a few minutes their drab and dreary lives would vanish as they participated vicariously in drama few men lived in reality. Snipe decided on the moment to give them what they wanted.

While the old marshal was still twenty paces away, he called out, "Howdy, Marshal Bill. We rescued Miss Libby and fetched her home. Me and my partner."

George Wakefield said, "He's lying, Bill. They're a pair of fast-talking sharpshooters. Ten days ago they tried to fleece me out of a thousand dollars on a dubious gold mine and I recognized them at once for what they are. They're crooks! I want them jailed. Lock them up. I insist!"

The crowd parted to let the marshal through to the stage, for stage it was, in the middle of the cross streets that cut the town into quarters. The crowd numbered over a hundred, and more were arriving with every minute.

"All in good time, George," Bill Butterworth said, and

faced the two desert men. The marshal was fully aware of the drama. Most of the mischief in town was the result of sheer boredom. "What's your story, men?"

"We—" Kestrel began, but Snipe silenced him with a hand on his arm. "Allow me, Kes."

Choosing the marshal as his audience of one, Snipe struck a dramatic pose. He would play the role of an Indian brave telling the tribal council the story of how he counted coup.

"Marshal, the moment me and my partner heard that the bank bandits were headed south into the desert some ten days ago, we said to ourselves that only true desert men could rescue the little girl. As you know, we were in the bank trying to negotiate a loan to buy a crusher and dry washer and some blasting powder. The banker saw fit to turn us down. We've got a rich little mine out there in the desert, marshal. The ore will run two ounces or better to the ton. You can actually see gold specks in the ore with the naked eye. But we can't get the ore out without blasting powder. And we can't crush it without a crusher. So when your banker refused us a loan and the bandits made off with the little girl, we elected to get her back to claim the reward."

He paused to eye the crowd. Every ear was tuned in. "We knew, if we had offered our help, that you would not have permitted us to go after the little girl for fear of danger to her life." He was getting warmed up. "So! Being true desert men, we slipped through your line of men and overtook the bandits the second night out.

"The bandits were much too confident, marshal! They knew that nobody without a great deal of water could cross the desert this time of the year and they were right! They had water kegs buried every twenty miles or so. They were so confident that there would be no pursuit, they neglected to post a sentry and they all went to sleep and then I . . . I, marshal, with the help of my worthy partner, crept in after dark and silently spirited the little girl away!"

He paused to let the audience savor the feat. Every man and boy in the crowd was living the moment.

"How did I do it? I slithered in on my belly, marshal. Right past nine sleeping bandits. When I found the little girl, I whispered in her ear. I whispered, 'Your daddy sent me to get you.' I told her not to make any noise. She is a smart little girl. She bravely told me that her legs were tied and the rope was made fast to a creosote bush. I slid down to her feet and cut the rope with my knife and whispered to the little girl to follow me. We crawled back through all them sleeping bandits. Nine of them, marshal! They had guns. Had they waked up, they would have shot us! But they didn't wake up, marshal, as I knew they would not, for I am a desert man. We slipped right past them nine vicious bandits and we got away!"

A wave of murmuring swept through the crowd.

"I tell you, marshal"—Snipe raised his voice so that it reached out to those on the fringe of the crowd—"it was not an easy thing to do! If only one of them bandits had waked up, he would have killed us both dead. Dead!"

He brought his voice back down. "But they didn't wake up, marshal. Not until we were fifty feet away did they wake up. Then they did, and they started shooting their guns! I scooped up the little girl, because she had no shoes, and I ran. I ran past my partner, who was waiting there with a spear. We ran away and found our burros and we ran some more. It was a close thing, marshal. They just about nabbed us. But we got away. Only because we're desert men. We know the desert, marshal. The desert is our home!" He stopped, seemingly exhausted, sucking in air.

Kestrel was thrilled to his toenails. He had known for years that Snipe was a storyteller, the way his father old William had been before him, but he had never dreamed that he'd witness a performance such as this. He was proud to call Snipe Morgan his partner and brother.

"Lies!" George Wakefield cried. "He's lying!"

With a dramatic gesture Snipe said, "Ask the little girl, marshal."

Silence. The only sound, the faint far-away thumping of a stamp mill, like the booming of distant drums, could be heard.

Then the little girl's voice was heard. "That's all true, Marshal Bill." And the crowd sighed.

George Wakefield raised his voice. "That was eight nights ago! Why didn't they come right back? They're lying. They tricked my daughter." He was desperately trying to save face.

Snipe spoke in his normal voice. "I followed the bandits after rescuing the little girl, naturally. They still had the money. Kestrel, my partner, took the little girl to a safe place and I followed the bandits. I stayed on their heels for three days and three nights, hoping I could take the money away from them." He paused. "Alas, I could not. They were too many for even me. I had no gun. The only weapons I had were my bow and my spears. I had to let them get away." He raised his hands, palms up, and lifting his shoulders he let them drop. "Not even a true desert man can lick nine bandits, desperate bandits with guns. But I tried! I tried, marshal." He sighed.

For the audience the performance was over. They longed to hear that the brave desert man, the small black man with the purple-grape eyes, had gone on to best the nine bandits. But it was not to be. They were only half satisfied. There wasn't a man or boy in the crowd who did not think that he, and only he, would have slaughtered the nine bandits and afterwards brought back the gold.

The marshal was talking to the banker, trying to reason with him. The crowd began to drift away. It was hot enough in the July sun to blister a rock. They went away reluctantly in little groups, talking, living again the great adventure.

The banker was proving bullheaded. He refused to accept the tale, even when his own daughter vouched for the truth of it.

The old marshal threw up his hands in disgust and turned from the banker to the two desert men. "I believe you, men," he said with an eloquent shrug. "But George Wakefield does not. Would you mind very much coming along to jail, where we can straighten this out?"

"Why should we mind, marshal?" Snipe said with open frankness. "If the man is such an ingrate, who am I to deny him his beliefs? Come along, partner. We're going to jail." He spoke loud enough for those citizens still within earshot to hear him.

Jack Shannon, who had listened with admiration and

utter disbelief to the tale, spoke up. "I'll take care of your wee burros, men. A fine bastard, that one is." And, taking the lead ropes, he swaggered out East Main Street toward the livery stable. The deputy had a keen political ear, and he could recognize a cover-up when he heard one.

Inside the combination office and jail the old marshal said to the two desert men. "I'll be damned if I'll lock up a pair of fine men such as you. Sit and I'll make you some coffee." He opened the street door again and poked his head out. Spotting one of the Prospect Scouts, he called out, "Peter! You, Peter Potts! Come here a minute. Run fetch Lawyer Stadd like a good boy. There's a nickel in it for you."

Turning from the door, he went to a potbellied heating stove on which sat a big blue-enamel coffee pot and banged the door open. He laid in kindling and wood and struck a lucifer with a fierce swipe and tossed it in. "Won't take long, men. Be right back." He took a bucket and went out and around to the pump and watering trough in front of the Prospect Mercantile Store.

The partners were alone. Snipe grinned like a jackass munching cholla cactus joints and Kestrel burst into uncontrollable laughter. He laughed until he got a stitch in his side and had to stop.

Snipe struck a pose and with one hand raised dramatically roared out, "It wasn't easy, marshal!" and Kestrel went into another laughing fit. They were sucking air, trying to stifle their risibles, when the old marshal returned.

The lawman poured water into the big coffee pot, took the pot to the door to throw the old grounds out into the street, and refilled the pot. He took a bag of Arbuckle's

Best Coffee down from a shelf and poured in a generous half pound and slapped the lid down. "There!" he said, as if he'd finally wrung George Wakefield's neck. He went around his desk to plop down and hoist his booted feet.

He eyed the two desert men for a moment and then said, "That was a masterful performance, mister. How'd you read what the crowd wanted to hear?"

In all innocence, Snipe said, "I don't quite get your meaning, marshal."

The marshal grinned. "You darkies are natural-born actors, ain'tcha? Never saw one yet who couldn't put on an act fit to jerk the tears out of a doorknob. Where's them bandits now?"

"I have no—" and Snipe stopped as the door opened to admit a short, paunchy man with plump cheeks and little raisin eyes.

"Thanks for coming, Elmer," the marshal said, rising to his feet. "Want you to meet a pair of jokers. Their last name is Morgan. Both of them. What's your first names, men?"

"Kestrel."

"Snipe."

"Well, this man is Elmer Stadd. He's a lawyer feller. He'll get you out of the fix, what little there is."

"Hello, men." The lawyer looked them up and down as if they were horses he might buy. "Heard you brought in George Wakefield's little girl. What's the problem, Bill?"

"Bullheaded George's got his ass in a crack, Elmer. He's still sticking to his belief that these here two men are members of the Blount Gang. A lot of bloody nonsense. I'll let the darky tell you the yarn."

Snipe didn't want any part of matching wits with the lawyer, so he took a position. "Before I tell anybody anything more, I want to know about the reward for fetching in the little girl. We do get a reward for that, don't we?"

The fat lawyer and the old marshal looked at each other, and at that moment Jack Shannon came in.

The old marshal said to his deputy, "Did George Wakefield get around to putting up a reward for his girl's safe return, Jack?"

"None that I heard about, Bill. There ought to be one though, by all rights. A man should be paid his due, me old dad always said." He winked at Snipe.

The wink and the tone of the deputy's words told Snipe volumes. He made a mental note of it, and said to the lawyer, "How do we go about collecting what's due us?"

The lawyer said, "There's no way you can collect, Mr. Morgan. There was no reward offered."

Snipe flared up with a mock showing of anger. "There's got to be a reward, dammit! We earned it! We risked our bygod necks getting that girl away from them bandits. What kind of man is that ingrate banker anyway?"

The lawyer answered. "Mr. Wakefield is a man whose wife was murdered. His bank was robbed. The wealthy husband and father of ten days ago is now a busted widower. I doubt if he could raise a fifty-dollar reward without going deeper into debt. You'll have to be reasonable, Mr. Morgan."

"Are you his lawyer or mine?" Snipe asked.

"I'm trying to be both, Mr. Morgan."

Snipe pretended to simmer down. He looked at Kestrel

and said with a note of resignation, "We busted our asses for nothing, partner."

Kestrel merely nodded.

"There is a reward for the capture of the bank robbers," the lawyer said. "Five hundred dollars. Contingent on the recovery of the stolen money, of course."

"Big deal," Snipe sneered. He looked at the marshal. "Are we under arrest?"

"I think not." The marshal silently consulted with his deputy, who shook his head no. "No, you're free to go any time you like, men."

"What the devil was I called in for if you're not going to charge them, Bill?" the lawyer asked.

"I sent for you before I made up my mind, Elmer."

"Come on, Kes, let's go," and Snipe headed for the door.

Kestrel looked at the coffee pot and licked his lips, longing for a mugful, then followed Snipe out.

Nobody tried to stop them. They left, but they hadn't gone five steps down the street when the deputy asked them to wait up. "I'll be showing you where your wee burros are, me friends."

As they were strolling out East Main Street, Snipe said, "I wonder just how much good it would do a deputy marshal to capture nine bandits?"

"I'm thinking it would be appreciated no end, me little friend," the deputy intoned.

The streets were all but deserted, it being Sunday. The stores were closed. Two blocks along and the deputy turned into the same livery barn where they had left the burros ten days ago. The beanpole liveryman and his beanpole son were mucking out a stall.

"I rationed them jackasses a measure of oats like you told me to, Mr. Jack," the oldest beanpole said. "Howdy, men. Heard you fetched back the little girl."

Snipe said, "Let's go back to the corral," and led the way. He went to the far corner and braced his back against the cornerpost. "I didn't tell the whole story, deputy."

"I was thinking you had not."

"And I could see you were thinking I had not," Snipe said, grinning. "Will you give us a couple of hours to get out of town?"

"You can have a month if you need it."

"The rest of the day and tonight will be enough."

"Done."

"Have you ever been out in the desert during the hot months?"

"No."

"It's a brutal master this time of the year. You could die out there."

"A man must die when the good Lord calls, Mr. Morgan."

"After you get to be marshal, where do you intend to go next?"

"The county needs a sheriff. It will be an elected office. From sheriff I will be the next governor. Politics is where the big money is. As governor I'll steal half the state. Naturally I will deny I ever said such a thing."

"Naturally, Governor." Snipe inclined his head. "And

capturing the bandits will give you a big boost up the political ladder. You're not expecting a share of the loot too, are you?"

"Me mind was wandering a bit along those lines."

"Will five thousand satisfy your larcenous soul?"

"I'll endeavor to make it do."

"Very well. You'll find the nine bandits at a place we call One Palm Spring. It's about a hundred miles or so to the south of here. You won't have any trouble capturing them, because I took away their guns. I killed three of their nine horses and their pack mule and ran off the other six horses. So they're on foot and their feet are inside riding boots. They won't be going any place soon. All you'll have to do is go take them, deputy."

"I'm thinking I'll be needing me a guide."

"We'll take you to within a mile of the spring. Will that suit you?"

"That will do me just fine, little friend. What will I be needing?"

"A good one-team wagon to start off with, with an extra pair of mules. Get a wagon with the same size wheels all around and take along a spare wheel in case one dries out on you. Grub for twenty days for twelve men. Water. Twenty ten-gallon whiskey kegs ought to do it. And nine pairs of leg shackles. Can you get all that together by tomorrow night?"

"I can."

"Good. Leave town after sundown tomorrow. We'll travel only at night. We'll be waiting for you about twenty miles directly south of here. You'll see our signal fire." Snipe held out his hand, and the next governor of the state took it. "No more scratching a poor man's butt, eh?"

"Me ass wasn't made to fit a poor man," the deputy said and swaggered away.

CHAPTER SIXTEEN

Deputy Marshal Jack Shannon had a lot of friends. When he left the livery stable, he went to the blacksmith shop of one of those friends and ordered nine pairs of leg shackles made. He wanted them before sundown the next day, he told his friend. The blacksmith went to work at once, asking no questions. He sacrificed church services to get the job done on time. He knew the Lord would understand.

A friendly tavern keeper supplied Jack with twenty ten-gallon whiskey kegs. A hardware merchant sold him a ten-foot length of heavy chain and a heavy brass padlock, both at cost. A friendly grocer put together a twenty-day supply of grub for twelve men. A wagonyard master furnished a sturdy wagon and four good mules. No questions were asked.

The next day Shannon told Bill Butterworth that he was taking a little trip.

The old marshal said, "You want me to know where you're going, Jack?"

"Bandit hunting," Jack said, and they left it at that.

After sundown Monday evening Jack Shannon drove

the loaded wagon west out of Prospect and turned off into the desert a mile out of town. He kept the North Star directly behind the wagon and traveled at a mule's pace until past midnight, when he spotted a signal fire ahead.

Since leaving the two desert men at the livery stable the day before, he'd been searching his brain for a way to take the bank loot away from them. He had come to the sad conclusion that there was no way, no way at all. Torture might do it, but he was dubious about even that. It was a pity, but he didn't brood about it. They would pay him the five thousand dollars. He knew they didn't have to do even that. Still, he reasoned that some day the two desert men just might need a friend in high office. So they would pay. He was certain of that.

When he arrived at the signal fire, there was nobody around, not that he could see. The quarter moon had been up for an hour; the desert landscape of creosote bush and bur sage looked empty for as far as he could see. There wasn't a bush big enough to hide behind.

He drew the team to a halt and stayed put on the wagon seat. Ten minutes or so later, the white desert man appeared as if he'd popped up out of the earth and said, "Hop down for a spell, deputy. Snipe will be here in a little bit. He's taking a look to see if you're being followed." The little white man was garbed like an Indian in leather breechclout and knee-high moccasins and wore a floppy-brimmed leather hat.

"You're wise not to be trusting me, Mr. Morgan," Shannon said as he hopped down and tied the team to a creosote bush, "for I am not a trustworthy man."

"You're in good company," the little man said. "Did you fetch along plenty of coffee?"

"Ten three-pound bags of Arbuckle's Best. Shall we be brewing up a pot?"

"That and some skillet bread if you've got plenty of wheat flour." Kestrel looked in the wagon. He counted four big wooden boxes packed with store-bought grub. "Looks good enough even for us rich folks, don't it?" He went around the back to look at the spare team of mules. They looked fit. He ticked off water kegs, shackles, grub. The spare wagon wheel. Satisfied, he gave a sharp whistle that carried a quarter mile in the stillness of the desert night. He lifted out a one-gallon-size blue-enamel coffee pot and went to work.

Kestrel had a big pot of corned-beef stew with Irish potatoes and canned tomatoes cooking, along with a big round loaf of skillet bread when Snipe showed up. Shannon had been watching the ears of the mules and knew about ten seconds before he saw the little black man that he was close by.

"I see you're no fool, deputy," Snipe said as he stepped into the yellow glow cast by the cookfire. "I saw you watching the mules for five minutes before I came in."

Shannon laughed. "What would you have done if I'd had some men following me?"

"Not a thing, deputy." Snipe hunkered down and reached for an enamel mug and the coffee pot. "We would have slipped silently away and you would be left holding an empty sack."

"I figured as much, Mr. Morgan. Where's your burros?"

"Up ahead a few miles."

Shannon smiled to himself. "For what it's worth, me fine little friends, you have this politician's promise he won't try any underhanded hanky-panky."

Kestrel dished up stew and broke off chunks of the delicious-smelling skillet bread.

"Have you thought about how you'll take the bandits?" Snipe asked. He was thinking ahead, as usual.

"What's there to think about?" Shannon said past a mouthful of stew. He swallowed. "You said you took their guns. They won't be any problem." His confidence in his ability was monumental.

"I wouldn't bet my life they don't have a gun." Snipe washed down a mouthful of skillet bread with coffee and sighed with pleasure. "I was in a bit of a rush when I gathered up their guns. I could have missed a pistol. Not a rifle. I got all of those."

"Just what were those nine men doing while you were taking their guns, me kinky-headed friend?" Shannon was trying to goad the little black man into saying something he didn't want to say.

"I reckon you'd say they were asleep." Snipe had used the same goading ploy himself a few times. "But that doesn't matter now, deputy. I'd hate to see a good man like you get a slug in your brisket. That's all."

Shannon grinned. "You kind of like me, don't you, you little black heathen?"

"I've come up on a lot worse," Snipe admitted. He filled the big man's coffee mug. "But let's stick to the subject in hand, Governor. If you try to take nine men by yourself, something might happen. You're not God, you know."

"Only his cousin." Shannon chuckled. "All right. What do you suggest I do?"

"I could lend you a hand."

"Doing what?" Shannon handed his enamel plate to Kestrel for a refill. He recognized the little white man as the choreboy of the partnership. His plate was helped without comment. The fire flared up for a second, lighting up the black man's face. The Irishman had never been around blacks; he knew this one better already than any he'd met, and he was singularly impressed.

"Well," Snipe said, "I could hold a rifle on the bandits while you shackle them. You can't do both at once."

"I was thinking of having them shackle each other. But yes, I'll accept your gracious offer. Snipe, is it? I'm Jack."

They shook hands. Shannon didn't offer to shake hands with Kestrel.

They broke camp, and the two desert men rode on the wagon to where the burros were staked out. When Snipe tried to get them to follow behind the wagon on long lead ropes, the little animals flatly refused. In the end Snipe rode on the wagon and Kestrel walked, leading the burros. Shannon thought it no more than fit and proper.

They traveled about thirty miles altogether that first night, and thirty miles on each of the two following nights. They made camp about ten miles north of One Palm Spring. By then the big Irishman and Snipe were good friends. Kestrel didn't mind; he wasn't jealous. He knew that Snipe would never play second best to any man. The two liked each other because they respected each other as equals.

After they had watered the four mules and two burros,

hobbled them, and had eaten and were lying in the shade of a clump of organpipe cactus, Snipe said to Kestrel, "Take the girls come night and head for Bull Quartz, partner. I'll show up in a day or two."

"That suits me, Snipe. I don't hanker to tangle with no nine bandits." Kestrel was trying to decide once and for all whether to go back to Alabama or go to Mexico with Snipe. He was leaning heavily in favor of Mexico. "Besides, I'm fed up with trying to stuff a certain black Irish glutton."

Shannon chuckled. "Watch your language, choreboy."

"I'm not afraid of you, you big horse turd. I'll sic Snipe on you."

The three men laughed and rolled over to catch some sleep.

Furnace-hot air settled around them. There was no breeze. Toward midday the air near the ground grew hotter still and dust devils formed and began dancing. Nothing stirred but an occasional bird flying high to get out of the heat. When the sun got directly overhead, they moved to the east side of the organpipes and sat under their hats until the cactus cast a shadow.

"How many years did you say you've lived out here in this devil's bake oven, Snipe?" Shannon asked as he tilted a one-gallon canteen and drained it dry.

"Six years, give or take."

"How can you bear it?"

"We like it. Don't we, Kes?"

"Yep."

"Is that gold mine of yours really rich or were you trying to fleece poor old Wakefield?"

"It's rich."

"But you won't be working it, right?"

"Maybe not. You want it?"

"What's it worth?"

"Oh, five thousand ought to be about the right price."

"I'll buy it. But not for cash. I'll need the five thousand to get it paying, so I can sell it for a million."

"What do you say, Kes? Do we sell it to him?"

"Take his note for ten thousand and it's his."

"Sold," Shannon said. "I won't give you any note, though. I'll give you my word as an Irish politician."

Snipe laughed. "That'll do us. Kes?"

"I'm satisfied. Be good to know we can call on a righteous Irish gentleman if we need a new grubstake someday."

Kestrel loaded the burros after first dark and left, headed west. Snipe and Shannon waited until after midnight before going on. The plan was for Snipe to work his way around to the west side of the spring by first daylight and Shannon was to go in past the spring on the east side. Snipe had Shannon's rifle and the big Irishman had his Navy Colt pistol. They would roust out the bandits and herd them under the saguaro-rib sun shelter and hold them there while they brought up the wagon.

The night was dark, the moon being a late-rising sickle. But the stars brightened the landscape well enough for Shannon to drive the mules around the occasional mesquite or paloverde or saguaro along the east side of Black Hill Three. Twice the mules spooked when encountering night-hunting rattlesnakes. Great horned owls hooted at them. The iron-shod wheels crunched on the desert pavement.

"Bear right."

They went on for another mile and Snipe said, "This ought to do it. We're about three hundred yards from the spring."

They unhitched the mules, hobbled them, and turned them loose.

"Take a canteen."

"Why?"

"Because the wise man never goes a hundred yards from camp in the desert without water. That's why."

Shannon took a canteen.

Snipe led the way. He took Shannon to within fifty feet of the spring and left him there. Snipe was to fire a shot as the signal to rush the bandits.

Going south about a hundred yards and then west, Snipe circled around the campsite that he knew so well, crossing the dry wash to work his way back up the slope. He settled down behind a black rock about fifty feet west of the sun shelter.

All this was not exactly to his liking. There were too many things that could go wrong. The bandits could be smarter than he'd given them credit for being. One of them could have made a bow and fashioned arrows. Or a spear. Or they might have a pistol. Or, perish the thought, they could have found the spot where he had buried their guns and were now as well armed as a troop of cavalry. He would have liked to observe them from the hilltop for a day or two. He had proposed doing just that, only to have Shannon question his courage. The trouble with getting killed was that it lasted such a long time.

One thing Snipe could do. He could wait for good daylight and get a look at the bandits first before giving the signal. Shannon had his faults, as do all men, but he would never put his partner in danger needlessly.

So Snipe waited. The eastern sky brightened and began casting a pink glow. He could make out the sun shelter. The hut. The pole in the center of the arrastra and the long arm. The doves were calling to each other. Another few minutes and the whole camp was light enough to make out small objects. He saw a pile of firewood that hadn't been there when he and Kestrel left some fifteen days before. He saw canteens hanging on the corner posts that held up the sun shelter. The bandits were still here.

He saw the first bandit. It was one of the young kids. Not the one he'd dunked in the water keg to bring him back to life. The kid came out of the grass-domed hut, went to the sun shelter, took down a canteen, and headed toward the spring.

Blount was the next bandit to show himself. He crawled out of the hut's low doorway and stood up to stretch and look around. He too went to the sun shelter for a canteen and headed for the spring. A morning ritual? It didn't matter.

Ten minutes later eight of the bandits were within Snipe's view. He waited, and when the ninth bandit did not show himself by good sunup, he took a deep breath, cocked the rifle, and fired a shot straight up. At once he jacked another shell into the chamber and yelled like a

Comanche as he rushed at the eight bandits, crying, "Hold it! Hold it!"

The bandits froze for a half second and then scattered like so many jackrabbits. Snipe was still rushing at them, whooping and yelling. "Stop! Halt!" But nobody stopped. They ran down the wash. They ran toward the spring. They ran in all directions. It was as though they had practiced doing just that. Snipe kept yelling, "Stop!" but it was useless. They kept going. And ten seconds after he'd fired the shot, he could see no bandits at all. They were all in hiding.

"Shannon! Shannon! They're getting away!"

Snipe had no recourse but to jump down in the arrastra and take aim at nothing. He wasn't about to shoot a bandit unless one threatened to take a shot at him. And he'd seen no guns.

About twenty seconds had gone by since the shot. He saw Shannon coming up from the spring, pushing a kid ahead of him and laughing fit to hogtie.

"They took you for a redskin, Snipe!" Shannon said between snorts of laughter. "I'd haul ass too if somebody black as coal dust and naked as a peeled skunk jumped out at me yelling like a scalded painter. Hey, men! Come on in! We won't shoot you!" His bellow echoed down the wash and up the slope where the saguaros lived. He shoved the cowering kid toward the sun shelter and said, "Stay put, kid."

Snipe stayed put too, down in the arrastra. He kept watch as Shannon stood spraddle-legged and called to the bandits to come in before they died of thirst. He kept laughing at Snipe between bellows.

"You scared the hair right off their pates, you bloody savage."

"I counted only eight, you big red ape." Snipe looked at the kid under the shelter. "Hey, kid, where's the other man?"

"There ain't . . . ain't but the eight of us, mister." The kid was still half scared to death.

"What happened to the ninth man?"

"He died off before we ever got here. Moss was his name.

"Any of the men down there got guns?"

"No, sir!"

Snipe climbed up out of the arrastra. The kid was too frightened to lie.

Shannon was still bellowing like a bull. "If you don't get your asses up here in ten seconds, I'll peel them off your rumps!"

The bandits showed themselves then; one, then two more, and soon all seven were coming in like cows at milking time. Shannon waved them toward the shelter with his Navy Colt. When they were all assembled, he said, "I'm the law. You're all under arrest for bank robbery and murder and child-taking. Don't be giving me no trouble now, me laddies." He grinned at Snipe. "You can go fetch the wagon now, chief."

Two hours later the eight men were shackled and the ten-foot length of heavy chain was run between their legs and padlocked to keep them together. They would have to stay like that until the spring furnished enough water to fill the empty water kegs. Only then could Shannon head back to Prospect. That would take about two days, for the spring's output was enough to fill only three kegs a day plus the water they needed to survive.

Snipe didn't take to the chore of cooking, but he did it anyway because he wanted to eat too. He made a big stew, baked three pones of skillet bread, and filled the big coffee pot twice to feed them all.

While Snipe was doing the cooking, Shannon talked to the bandits. The question he kept asking over and over again was, "Where did you hide the bank loot?"

The answer was always the same. Pointing at Snipe, they said, "That little black bastard made off with it."

"Stop lying, you idiots! Where'd you hide the bloody loot?"

That went on until the bandits got the message. Then one of them said, "We don't know, mister. We lost it somewheres."

"That's better," Shannon told them, and left them alone.

At midday Shannon asked Snipe to go with him to the spring. There Snipe looked up at the palm for the chulas. They were not there. The bandits had killed them to eat. That hurt Snipe. For a moment he hated the bandits, for the first and only time.

"Well, you old crowbait," Shannon said to him there under the fan palm tree. "I'll have them properly trained by the time I get them to Prospect. They'll swear on their dear mothers' graves they lost the loot. Now, me little friend, wouldn't you say it's time you went and got me money?"

Snipe shook his head. "I could, Jack. But wouldn't it be better if I sent it to you by Wells Fargo?"

The big Irishman grinned and gave him a swat on his back. "By all that's holy, Snipe Morgan. You're the smartest black Irishman I've ever met." It was the highest compliment the deputy could give the little black desert man, and Snipe grinned his acceptance as if it was his just due.